His male brain and body were very attentive to Livvy's ample curves and that barely there white lace bra she was wearing, visible under her rain-soaked shirt.

As if she'd realized where his attention was, her gaze dropped down to her chest. "Oh!" leaped from her mouth. And she slapped the large manila envelope over the now transparent shirt. She also got in the truck. Fast. She slammed the door.

"You could have said something," she mumbled.

"I could have," he admitted, "but let's just say I was dumbfounded and leave it at that."

Reed didn't want to defend himself, but her continuing stare prompted him to say something. "Hey, just because I wear this badge, it doesn't mean I'm not a red-blooded male."

"Great. This won't be a problem."

"*This?*"

"Your male red blood."

Well, that put him in his place and would make these next three days protecting her, trying to solve the case, much easier.

Parts of his body disagreed.

DELORES FOSSEN

SHOTGUN SHERIFF

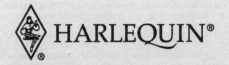

HARLEQUIN®

TORONTO • NEW YORK • LONDON
AMSTERDAM • PARIS • SYDNEY • HAMBURG
STOCKHOLM • ATHENS • TOKYO • MILAN • MADRID
PRAGUE • WARSAW • BUDAPEST • AUCKLAND

ISBN-13: 978-0-373-69453-2

SHOTGUN SHERIFF

ABOUT THE AUTHOR

Imagine a family tree that includes Texas cowboys, Choctaw and Cherokee Indians, a Louisiana pirate and a Scottish rebel who battled side by side with William Wallace. With ancestors like that, it's easy to understand why Texas author and former air force captain Delores Fossen feels as if she was genetically predisposed to writing romances. Along the way to fulfilling her DNA destiny, Delores married an air force top gun who just happens to be of Viking descent. With all those romantic bases covered, she doesn't have to look too far for inspiration.

Books by Delores Fossen

HARLEQUIN INTRIGUE
990—UNDERCOVER DADDY*
1008—STORK ALERT*
1026—THE CHRISTMAS CLUE*
1044—NEWBORN CONSPIRACY*
1050—THE HORSEMAN'S SON*
1075—QUESTIONING THE HEIRESS
1091—SECURITY BLANKET**
1110—BRANDED BY THE SHERIFF†
1116—EXPECTING TROUBLE†
1122—SECRET DELIVERY†
1144—SHE'S POSITIVE
1163—CHRISTMAS GUARDIAN**
1186—SHOTGUN SHERIFF

*Five-Alarm Babies
**Texas Paternity
†Texas Paternity: Boots and Booties

CAST OF CHARACTERS

Sheriff Reed Hardin—As sheriff of Comanche Creek, he's reluctant to cast his lot with the Texas Rangers because he wants to conduct his own investigation into the town's recent string of murders.

Sgt. Olivia "Livvy" Hutton—The Rangers' CSI who's as suspicious of Reed as he is of her.

Marcie James—A records clerk that someone obviously wanted to silence. Now, Livvy and Reed must work together to find her killer.

Jonah Becker—A powerful rancher who's not afraid to use his money to get what he wants. Is he a cold-blooded killer or just an unscrupulous businessman?

Woodrow "Woody" Sadler—The popular mayor who might have greased the way for Jonah to profit from a shady land deal.

Deputy Shane Tolbert—Marcie's ex who's arrested for her murder. They had a checkered relationship. Despite being a small-town lawman, he's well trained in forensics.

Billy Whitley—The city official who might have done something illegal to orchestrate the land deal that's under investigation.

Charla Whitley—Billy's wife. Did she kill Marcie to hide her own wrongdoing?

Jerry Collier—Head of the land office and Marcie's former boss. He's also connected to the illegal sale of Native American artifacts that were recovered after Jonah got the land.

Ben Tolbert—Shane's father. He wants his son cleared of all charges, but how far is he willing to go to make sure that neither Shane nor he spends any time in jail?

Chapter One

Comanche Creek, Texas

Something was wrong.

Sheriff Reed Hardin eased his Smith and Wesson from his leather shoulder holster and stepped out of his mud-scabbed pickup truck. The heels of his rawhide boots sank in the rain-softened dirt. He lifted his head. Listened.

It was what he *didn't* hear that bothered him.

Yeah, something was definitely wrong.

There should have been squawks from the blue jays or the cardinals. Maybe even a hawk in search of its breakfast. Instead there was only the unnerving quiet of the Texas Hill Country woods sardined with thick mesquites, hackberries and thorny underbrush that bulged thick and green with spring growth. Whatever had scared off the birds could be lurking in there. Reed was hoping for a coyote or some other four-legged predator because the alternative put a knot in his gut.

After all, just hours earlier a woman had been murdered a few yards from here.

With his gun ready and aimed, Reed made his way

up the steep back path toward the cabin. He'd chosen the route so he could look around for any evidence he might have missed when he'd combed the grounds not long after the body had been discovered. He needed to see if anything was out of place, anything that would help him make sense of this murder. So far, nothing.

Except for his certainty that something was wrong.

And he soon spotted proof of it.

There were footprints leading down and then back up the narrow trail. Too many of them. There should have been only his and his deputy's, Kirby Spears, since Reed had given firm orders that all others use the county road just a stone's throw from the front of the cabin. He hadn't wanted this scene contaminated and there were signs posted ordering No Trespassers.

He stooped down and had a better look at the prints. "What the hell?" Reed grumbled.

The prints were small and narrow and with a distinctive narrow cut at the back that had knifed right into the gray-clay-and-limestone dirt mix.

Who the heck would be out here in high heels?

He thought of the dead woman, Marcie James, who'd been found shot to death in the cabin about fourteen hours earlier. Marcie hadn't been wearing heels. Neither had her alleged killer. And Reed should know because the alleged killer was none other than his own deputy, Shane Tolbert.

Cursing the fact that Shane was now locked up in a jail he used to police with Reed and Kirby, Reed elbowed aside a pungent dew-coated cedar branch and hurried up the hill. It didn't take him long to see more evidence of his something-was-wrong theory. There were no signs of his deputy or the patrol car.

However, there was a blonde lurking behind a sprawling oak tree.

Correction. An *armed* blonde. A stranger, at that.

She was tall, at least five-ten, and dressed in a long-sleeved white shirt that she'd tucked into the waist of belted dark jeans. Her hair was gathered into a sleek ponytail, not a strand out of place. And yep, there were feminine heels on her fashionable black boots. But her attire wasn't what Reed focused on. It was that lethal-looking Sig-Sauer Blackwater pistol gripped in her latex-gloved right hand. She had it aimed at the cabin.

Reed aimed his Smith and Wesson at her.

Maybe she heard him or sensed he was there because her gaze whipped in his direction. She shifted her position a fraction, no doubt preparing to turn her weapon on him, but she stopped when her attention landed on the badge Reed had clipped to his belt. Then, she did something that surprised the heck out of him.

She put her left index finger to her mouth in a *shhh* gesture.

Reed glanced around, trying to make sense of why she was there and why in Sam Hill she'd just shushed him as if she'd had a right to do it. He didn't see anyone other than the blonde, but she kept her weapon trained on the cabin.

He walked closer to her, keeping his steps light, just in case there was indeed some threat other than this woman. If so, then someone had breached a crime scene because the cabin was literally roped off with yellow crime-scene tape. And with the town's gossip mill in full swing, there probably wasn't anyone within fifty miles of Comanche Creek who hadn't heard about the latest murder.

Emphasis on the word *latest*.

Everyone knew to keep away or they'd have to deal with him. He wasn't a badass—most days, anyway—but people usually did as he said when he spelled things out for them. And he always spelled things out.

"I'm Sheriff Reed Hardin," he grumbled when he got closer.

"Livvy Hutton."

Like her face, her name wasn't familiar to him. Who the devil was she?

She tipped her head towards the cabin. "I think someone's inside."

Well, there sure as hell shouldn't be. "Where's my deputy?"

"Running an errand for me."

That didn't improve Reed's mood. He was about to question why his deputy would be running an errand for an armed woman in fancy boots, but she shifted her position again. Even though she kept her attention nailed to the cabin, he could now see the front of her white shirt.

The sun's rays danced off the distinctive star badge pinned to it.

"You're a Texas Ranger?" he asked.

He hadn't intended for that to sound like a challenge, but it did. Reed couldn't help it. He already had one Ranger to deal with, Lieutenant Wyatt Colter, who'd been in Comanche Creek for days, since the start of all this mess that'd turned his town upside-down. Now, he apparently had another one of Texas's finest. That was two too many for a crime scene he planned to finish processing himself. He had a plan for this investigation, and that plan didn't include Rangers.

"Yes. Sergeant Olivia Hutton," she clarified. "CSI for the Ranger task force."

She spared him a glance from ice-blue eyes. Not a friendly glance either. That brief look conveyed a lot of displeasure.

And skepticism.

Reed had seen that look before. He was a small-town Texas sheriff, and to some people that automatically made him small-minded, stupid and incapable of handling a capital murder investigation. That attitude was one of the reasons for the so-called task force that included not only Texas Rangers but a forensic anthropologist and apparently this blonde crime-scene analyst.

As he'd done with Lieutenant Colter, the other Ranger, Reed would set a few ground rules with Sergeant Hutton. Later, that was. For now, he needed to figure out if anyone was inside the cabin. That was at the top of his mental list.

Reed didn't see anyone near either of the two back curtainless windows. Nor had the crime-scene tape been tampered with. It was still in place. Of course, someone could have ducked beneath it and gotten inside—after they'd figured out a way to get past the locked windows and doors. Other than the owner and probably some members of the owner's family, Reed and his deputy were the only ones with keys.

"Did you actually see anyone in the cabin?" he asked in a whisper.

She turned her head, probably so she could whisper as well, but the move put them even closer. Practically mouth to cheek. Not good. Because with all that closeness, he caught her scent. Her perfume was high-end, but that was definitely chocolate on her breath.

"I heard something," she explained. "Your deputy and I were taking castings of some footprints we found over there." She tipped her head to a cluster of trees on the east side of the cabin. "I wanted to get them done right away because it's supposed to rain again this afternoon."

Yeah, it was, and if they'd been lucky enough to find footprints after the morning and late-night drizzle, then they wouldn't be there long.

"After Deputy Spears left to send the castings to your office," she continued, "I turned to go back inside. That's when I thought I heard someone moving around in there."

Reed took in every word of her account. *Every word.* But he also heard the accent. Definitely not a Texas drawl. He was thinking East Coast and would find out more about that later. For now, he might have an intruder on his hands. An intruder who was possibly inside with a cabin full of potential evidence that could clear Shane's name. Or maybe it was the cabin's owner, Jonah Becker, though Reed had warned the rancher to stay far away from the place.

With his gun still aimed, Reed stepped out a few inches from the cover of the tree. "This is Sheriff Hardin," he called out. "If anyone's in there, get the hell out here now."

Beside him, Livvy huffed. "You think that's wise, to stand out in the open like that?"

He took the time to toss her a scowl. "Maybe it'd be a dumb idea in Boston, but here in Comanche Creek, if there's an intruder, it's likely to be someone who knows to do as I say."

He hoped.

"Not Boston," she snarled. "New York."

He gave her a flat look to let her know that didn't make things better. A Texas Ranger should damn well be born and raised in Texas. And she shouldn't wear high-heeled boots.

Or perfume that reminded him she was a woman.

Reed knew that was petty, but with four murders on his hands, he wasn't exactly in a generous mood. He extended that non-generous mood to anyone who might be inside that cabin.

"Get out here!" he shouted. And by God, it better happen now.

Nothing. Well, nothing except Livvy's spurting breath and angry mumbles.

"Just because the person doesn't answer you, it doesn't mean the place is empty," she pointed out.

Yeah. And that meant he might have a huge problem. He didn't want the crime scene compromised, and he didn't want to shoot anyone. *Yet.*

"How long were Deputy Spears and you out there casting footprints?" he asked.

"A half hour. And before that we were looking around in the woods."

That explained how her footprints had gotten on the trail. The castings and the woods search also would have given someone plenty of time to get inside. "I'm guessing Deputy Spears unlocked the cabin for you?"

The sergeant shook her head. "It wasn't necessary. Someone had broken the lock on a side window, apparently crawled in and then opened the front door from the inside."

Reed cursed. "And you didn't see that person when you went in?"

Another head shake that sent her ponytail swishing. "The place was empty when I first arrived. I checked every inch," she added, cutting off his next question: *Was she sure about that?*

So, he had possibly two intruders. Great. Dealing with intruders wasn't on his to-do list today.

Now, he cursed himself. He should have camped out here, but he hadn't exactly had the manpower to do that with just him and two deputies, including the one behind bars. He'd had to process Shane's arrest and interrogate him. He had been careful. He'd done everything by the book so no one could accuse him of tampering with anything that would ultimately clear Shane's name. Kirby Spears had guarded the place until around midnight, but then Reed and he had had to respond to an armed robbery at the convenience store near the interstate.

Lately, life in Comanche Creek had been far from peaceful and friendly—even though that was what it said on the welcome sign at the edge of the city limits. Before the spring, it'd been nearly a decade since there'd been a murder. Now, there'd been four.

Four!

And because some of those bodies had been dumped on Native American burial ground, the whole town felt as if it were sitting on a powder keg. With the previous murder investigations and the latest one, Reed was operating on a one-hour nap, too much coffee and a shorter fuse than usual.

He glanced around. "How'd you get up here?" he asked the sergeant. "Because I didn't see a vehicle."

"I parked at the bottom of the hill just off the county road. I wanted to get a good look at the exterior of the crime scene before I went inside." She glanced around as well. "How'd you get up here?" she asked him.

"I parked on the back side of the hill." And for the same reason. Of course, that didn't mean they were going to see eye-to-eye on anything else. Reed was betting this would get ugly fast.

"Reed?" someone called out, the sound coming from the cabin.

Reed cursed some more because he recognized that voice. He lowered his gun, huffed and strolled toward the front door. It swung open just as Reed stepped onto the porch, and he came face-to-face with his boss, Mayor Woody Sadler. His friend. His mentor. As close to a father as Reed had ever had since his own dad had died when Reed was seven years old.

But Woody shouldn't have been within a mile of the place.

Surrogate fatherhood would earn Woody a little more respect than Reed would give others, but even Woody wasn't going to escape a good chewing-out. And maybe even more.

"What are you doing here?" Livvy demanded, taking the words right out of Reed's mouth. Unlike Reed, she didn't lower her gun. She pointed the Blackwater right at Woody.

Woody eased off his white Stetson, and the rattler tail attached to the band gave a familiar hollow jangle. He nodded a friendly greeting.

He didn't get anything friendly in return.

"This is Woody Sadler. The mayor of Comanche

Creek," Reed said, making introductions. "And this is Sergeant Livvy Hutton. A Texas Ranger from New York."

Woody's tired gray eyes widened. Then narrowed, making the corners of his eyes wrinkle even more than they already were. Obviously he wasn't able to hold back a petty reaction either. "New York?"

"Spare me the jokes. I was born in a small town near Dallas. Raised in upstate New York." As if she'd declared war on it, Livvy shoved her gun back into her shoulder holster and barreled up the steps. "And regardless of where I'm from, this is my crime scene, and you were trespassing," she declared to Woody and then fired a glance at Reed to declare it to him as well.

"I didn't touch anything," Woody insisted.

Livvy obviously didn't take his word for it. She bolted past Woody, grabbed her equipment bag from the porch and went inside.

"I swear," Woody added to Reed. "I didn't touch a thing."

Reed studied Woody's body language. The stiff shoulders. The sweat popping out above his top lip. Both surefire signs that the man was uncomfortable about something. "You're certain about that?"

"I'm damn certain." The body language changed. No more nerves, just a defensive stare that made Reed feel like a kid again. Still, that didn't stop Reed from doing his job.

"Then why didn't you answer when I called out?" Reed asked. "And why'd you break the lock on the window and go in there?"

"I didn't hear you calling out, that's why, and I didn't break any lock. The door was wide open when I got here about fifteen minutes ago." There was another shift in body language. Woody shook his head and wearily ran his hand through his thinning salt-and-pepper hair. "I just had to see for myself. I figured there'd be something obvious. Something that'd prove that Shane didn't do this."

Reed blew out a long breath. "I know. I want to prove Shane's innocence, too, but this isn't the way to go about doing it. If there's proof and the New York Ranger finds it, she could say you planted it there."

Woody went still. Then, he cursed. "I wouldn't do that."

"I believe you. But Sergeant Olivia Hutton doesn't know you from Adam."

Woody's gaze met his. "She's gunning for Shane?"

Probably. For Shane and anyone who thought he was innocent. But Reed kept that to himself. "Best to let me handle this," he insisted. "I'll talk to you when I'm back in town. Oh, and see about hiring me a temporary deputy or two."

Woody bobbed his head, slid back on his Stetson and ambled off the porch and down the hill, where he'd likely parked. Reed waited until he was sure the mayor was on his way before he took another deep breath and went inside.

He only made it two steps.

Livvy threw open the door. "Where's the mayor?" she demanded.

"Gone." Reed hitched his thumb toward the downside of the hill. "Why?"

Her hands went on her hips, and those ice-blue eyes turned fiery hot. "Because he stole some evidence, that's why, and I intend to arrest him."

Chapter Two

Livvy was in full stride across the yard when the sheriff caught up with her, latched on to her arm, whirled her around and brought her to an abrupt halt.

"I'm arresting him," she repeated and tried to throw off his grip.

She would probably have had better luck wrestling a longhorn to the ground. Despite Sheriff Reed Hardin's lanky build, the man was strong. And angry. That anger was stamped on his tanned face and in his crisp green eyes.

"I don't care if Woody Sadler is your friend." She tried again to get away from the sheriff's clamped hand. "He can't waltz in here and steal evidence that might be pertinent to a murder investigation."

"Just hold on." He pulled out his cell phone from his well-worn Wranglers, scrolled through some numbers and hit the call button. "Woody," he said when the mayor apparently answered, "you need to get back up here to the cabin right now. We might have a problem."

"Might?" Livvy snarled when Sheriff Hardin ended the call. "Oh, we *definitely* have a problem. Tampering with a crime scene is a third-degree felony."

The sheriff dismissed that with a headshake. "Woody's the mayor, along with being a law-abiding citizen. He didn't tamper with anything. You said yourself that someone had broken the lock, and Woody didn't do that."

"Well, he obviously isn't so law-abiding because he walked past crime-scene tape and entered without permission or reason."

"He had reason," Reed mumbled. "He's worried about Shane. And sometimes worried people do dumb things." He looked down at the chokehold he had on her arm, mumbled something indistinguishable, and his grip melted away. "What exactly is missing?"

"A cell phone." Livvy tried to go after the trespassing mayor again, but Reed stepped in front of her. Worse, her forward momentum sent her slamming right against his chest. Specifically, her breasts against his chest. The man was certainly solid. There were lots of corded muscles in his chest and abs.

Both of them cursed this time.

And Livvy shook her head. She shouldn't be noticing anything that intimate about a man whom she would likely end up at odds with. She shouldn't be noticing his looks, either. Those eyes. The desperado stubble on his strong square jaw and the tousled coffee-brown hair that made him look as if he'd just crawled out of bed.

Or off a poster for a Texas cowboy-sheriff.

It was crystal-clear that he didn't want her anywhere near the crime scene or his town. Tough. Livvy had been given a job to do, and she *never* walked away from the job.

Sheriff Hardin would soon learn that about her.

By God, she hadn't fought her way into the Ranger

organization to be stonewalled by some local yokels who believed one of their own could do no wrong.

"What cell phone?" Reed asked.

Because the adrenaline and anger had caused her breath and mind to race, it took her a moment to answer. First, she glanced at the road and saw the mayor inching his way back up toward them. "One I found in the fireplace when I was going through the front room. You no doubt missed it in the initial search because the ashes were covering it completely. The only reason I found it is because I ran a metal detector over the place to search for any spent shell casings. Then, I photographed it, bagged it and put it on the table. It's missing."

His jaw muscles stirred. "It's Marcie's phone?"

"I don't know. I showed it to Deputy Spears, and he said he didn't think it was Shane's. That means it could be Marcie's."

"Or the killer's."

She was certain her jaw muscles stirred, too. "Need I remind you that you found Deputy Shane Tolbert standing over Marcie's body, and he had a gun in his hand? Marcie was his estranged lover. I hate to state the obvious, but all the initial evidence indicates that Shane *is* the killer."

Livvy instantly regretted spouting that verdict. It wasn't her job to get a conviction or jump to conclusions. She was there to gather evidence and find the truth, and she didn't want anything, including her anger, to get in the way.

"Shane said he didn't kill her," Reed explained. His voice was calm enough, but not his eyes. Everything else about him was unruffled except for those intense green eyes. They were warrior eyes. "He said Marcie called him and asked him to meet her at the cabin. The moment he stepped inside, someone hit him over the head, and he fell on the floor. When he came to, Marcie was dead and someone had put a gun in his hand."

Yes, she'd already heard the summary of Shane's statement from Deputy Kirby Spears. Livvy intended to study the interrogation carefully, especially since Reed had been the one to question the suspect.

Talk about a conflict of interest.

Still, in a small town like Comanche Creek, Reed probably hadn't had an alternative, especially since the on-scene Ranger, Lieutenant Colter, had been called back to the office. If Reed hadn't questioned Shane, then it would have been left to his junior deputy, Kirby, who was greener than the Hill Country's spring foliage.

The mayor finally made his way toward them and stopped a few feet away. "What's wrong?"

"Where's the cell phone that I'd bagged and tagged?" Livvy asked, not waiting for Reed to respond.

Woody Sadler first looked at Reed. Then, her. "I have no idea. I didn't take it."

"Then you won't mind proving that to me. Show me your pockets."

Woody hesitated, until Reed gave him a nod. It wasn't exactly a cooperative nod, either, and the accompanying grumble had a get-this-over-with tone to it.

The mayor pulled out a wallet from the back pocket of his jeans and a handkerchief and keys from the front ones. No cell phone, but that didn't mean he hadn't taken it. The man had had at least ten minutes to discard it along the way up or down the hill to his vehicle.

"Taking the cell won't help your friend's cause," she pointed out. "I already phoned in the number, and it'll be traced."

Woody lifted his shoulder. "Good. Because maybe what you learn about that phone will get Shane out of jail. He didn't kill Marcie."

Reed stared at her. "Can the mayor go now, or do you intend to strip-search him?"

Livvy ignored that swipe and glanced down at Woody's snakeskin boots. "You wear about a size eleven." She turned her attention to Reed. "And so do you. That looks to be about the size of the footprints that I took casts of over in the brush."

"So?" Woody challenged.

"So, the location of those prints means that someone could have waited there for Marcie to arrive. They could be the footprints of the killer. Or the killer's accomplice if he had one. Sheriff Hardin would have had reason to be out here, but what about you? Before this morning, were you here at the cabin in the past forty-eight hours?"

"No." The mayor's answer was quick and confident.

Livvy didn't intend to take his word for it.

"You can go now," Reed told the mayor.

Woody slid his hat back on, tossed her a glare and delivered his parting shot from over his shoulder as he walked away. "You might do to remember that Reed is the law in Comanche Creek."

Livvy could have reminded him that she was there on orders from the governor, but instead she took out her binoculars from her field bag and watched Woody's exit. If he stopped to pick up a discarded cell phone, she would arrest him on the spot.

"He didn't take that phone," Reed insisted.

"Then who did?"

"The real killer. He could have done it while Kirby and you were casting the footprints."

"The real killer," she repeated. "And exactly who would that be?"

"Someone that Marcie got involved with in the past two years when she was missing and presumed dead."

Livvy couldn't discount that. After all, Marcie had faked her own death so she wouldn't have to testify against a powerful local rancher who'd been accused of bribing officials in order to purchase land that the Comanche community considered their own. The rancher, Jonah Becker, who also owned this cabin, could have silenced Marcie when she returned from the grave.

Or maybe the killer was someone who'd been furious that Marcie hadn't gone through with her testimony two years ago. There were several people who could have wanted the woman dead, but Shane was the one who'd been found standing over her body.

"See? He didn't take the cell phone," Reed grumbled when the mayor didn't stop along the path to retrieve anything he might have discarded. The mayor got into a shiny fire-engine-red gas-guzzler of a truck and sped away, the massive tires kicking up a spray of mud and gravel.

"He could be planning to come back for it later," Livvy commented. But probably not. He would have known that she would search the area.

"Instead of focusing on Woody Sadler," Reed continued, "how about taking a look at the evidence inside the cabin? Because naming Shane as the primary suspect just doesn't add up."

Ah, she'd wondered how long it would take to get to this subject. "How do you figure that?"

"For one thing, I swabbed Shane's hands, and there was no gunshot residue. Plus, this case might be bigger than just Shane and Marcie. You might not have heard, but a few days ago there were some other bodies that turned up at the Comanche burial grounds."

"I heard," she said. "I also heard their eyes were sealed with red paint and ochre clay. In other words, a Native American ritual. There's nothing Native American or ritualistic about this murder."

Still, that didn't mean the deaths weren't connected. It just meant she didn't see an immediate link. The only thing that was glaring right now was Deputy Shane Tolbert's involvement in this and his sheriff's need to defend him.

Livvy started the walk down the hill to look for that missing phone. Thankfully, it was silver and should stand out among the foliage. And then she remembered the note in her pocket with the cell number on it. She took out her own phone and punched in the numbers to call the cell so it would ring.

She heard nothing.

Just in case it was buried beneath debris or something, she continued down the hill, listening for it.

Reed followed her, of course.

Livvy would have preferred to do this search alone because the sheriff was turning out to be more than a nuisance. He was a distraction. Livvy blamed that on his too-good looks and her stupid fantasies about cowboys. She'd obviously watched too many Westerns growing up, and she reminded herself that in almost all cases the fantasy was much hotter than the reality.

She glanced at Reed again and mentally added *maybe not in this case.*

In those great-fitting jeans and equally great-fitting blue shirt, he certainly looked as if he could compete with a fantasy or two.

When she felt her cheeks flush, Livvy quickly got her mind on something else—the job. It was obvious that the missing cell wasn't ringing so she ended the call and put her own cell back in her pocket. Instead of listening for the phone, she'd just have to hope that the mayor had turned it off but still tossed it in a place where she could spot it.

"The mayor's not guilty," Reed tried again. "And neither is Shane."

She made a sound of disagreement. "Maybe there was no GSR on his hands because Shane wore gloves when he shot her," she pointed out. Though Livvy was certain Reed had already considered that.

"There were no gloves found at the scene."

She had an answer for that as well. "He could have discarded them and then hit himself over the head to make it look as if he'd been set up."

"Then he would have had to change his clothes, too, because there was no GSR on his shirt, jeans, belt, watch, badge, holster or boots."

"You tested all those items for gunshot residue?"

"Yeah, I did," he snapped. "This might be a small town, Sergeant Hutton, but we're not idiots. Shane and I have both taken workshops on crime-scene processing, and we keep GSR test kits in the office."

It sounded as if Sheriff Hardin had been thorough, but she would reserve judgment on whether he'd learned enough in those workshops.

"But Shane was holding the murder weapon, right?" Livvy clarified.

"Appears to have been, but it wasn't his gun. He says he has no idea who it belongs to. The bullet taken from Marcie's body is on the way to the lab for comparison, and we're still searching the databases to try to figure out the owner of the gun."

Good. She'd call soon and press for those results and the plaster castings of the footprints. Because the sooner she finished this crime scene, the sooner she could get out of here and head back to Austin. She didn't mind small towns, had even grown up in one, but this small town—and its sheriff—could soon get to her.

Livvy continued to visually comb the right side of the path, and when they got to the bottom, they started back up while she examined the opposite side. There was no sign of a silver phone.

Mercy.

She didn't want to explain to her boss how she'd let possible crucial evidence disappear from a crime scene that she was working. She had to find that phone or else pray the cell records could be accessed.

"What about the blood spatter in the cabin?" Reed asked, grabbing her attention again.

"I'm not finished processing the scene yet." In fact, she'd barely started though she had already spent nearly an hour inside. She had hours more, maybe days, of work ahead of her. Those footprint castings had taken priority because they could have been erased with just a light rain. "But in my cursory check, I didn't see any spatter, only the blood pool on the floor. Since Marcie was shot at point-blank range, that doesn't surprise me. Why? Did you find blood spatter?"

"No. But if Shane's account is true about someone clubbing him over the back of the head, then there might be some. He already had a head injury, and it had been aggravated with what looked like a second blow. But the wood's dark-colored, and I didn't want to spray the place with Luminol since I read it can sometimes alter small droplets. Judging from the wound on Shane's head, we'd be looking for a very small amount because the gash was only about an inch across."

She glanced at him and hoped she didn't look too surprised. Most non-CSI-trained authorities would have hosed down the place with Luminol, the chemical to detect the presence of biological fluids, and would have indeed compromised the pattern by causing the blood to run. That in turn, could compromise critical evidence.

"What?" he asked.

Livvy walked ahead of him, up the steps and onto the porch and went inside the cabin. "Nothing."

"Something," Reed corrected, following her. He shut the door and turned on the overhead lights. "You'd dismissed me as just a small-town sheriff."

"No." She shrugged. "Okay, maybe. Sorry."

"Don't be. I dismissed you, too."

Since her back was to him, she smiled. For a moment. "Still do?"

"Not because of your skill. You seem to know what

you're doing. But I'm concerned you won't do everything possible to clear Shane's name."

"And I'm concerned you'll do anything to clear it."

He made a sound of agreement that rumbled deep in his throat. "I can live with a stalemate if I know you'll be objective."

The man certainly did know how to make her feel guilty. And defensive. "The evidence is objective, and my interpretation of it will be, too. Don't worry. I'll check for that blood spatter in just a minute."

Riled now about the nerve he'd hit, she grabbed a folder from her equipment bag. "First though, I'd like to know if it wasn't Woody Sadler, then who might have compromised the crime scene and stolen the phone." She slapped the folder on the dining table and opened it. Inside were short bios of persons of any possible interest in this case.

Reed's bio was there on top, and Livvy had already studied it.

He was thirty-two, had never been married and had been the sheriff of Comanche Creek for eight years. Before that, he'd been a deputy. His father, also sheriff, had been killed in the line of duty when Reed was seven. Reed's mother had fallen apart after her husband's murder and had spent the rest of her short life in and out of mental institutions before committing suicide. And the man who'd raised Reed after that was none other than the mayor, Woody Sadler.

She could be objective about the evidence, but she seriously doubted that Reed could ever be impartial about the man who'd raised him.

Livvy moved Reed's bio aside. The mayor's. And

Shane's. "Who would be bold or stupid enough to walk into this cabin and take a phone with me and your deputy only yards away?"

Reed thumbed through the pages, extracted one and handed it to her. "Jonah Becker. He's the rancher Marcie was supposed to testify against. He probably wouldn't have done this himself, but he could have hired someone if he thought that phone would link him in any way to Marcie."

Yes. Jonah Becker was a possibility. Reed added the bio for Jonah's son. And Jerry Collier, the man who ran the Comanche Creek Land Office. Then Billy Whitley, a city official. The final bio that Reed included was for Shane's father, Ben Tolbert. He was another strong possibility since he might want to protect his son.

"I'll question all of them," Reed promised.

"And I'll be there when you do," Livvy added. She heard the irritation in his under-the-breath grumble, but she ignored him, took the handheld UV lamp from her bag and put on a pair of monochromatic glasses.

"Shane said he was here when he was hit." Reed pointed to the area in front of the fireplace. It was only about three feet from where Marcie's body had been discovered.

Livvy walked closer, her heels echoing on the hardwood floor. The sound caused Reed to eye her boots, and again she saw some questions about her choice of footwear.

"They're more comfortable than they look," she mumbled.

"They'd have to be," he mumbled back.

Though comfort wasn't exactly the reason she was

wearing them. She'd just returned from a trip to visit her father, and one of her suitcases—the one that contained her favorite work boots—had been lost. There'd been no time to replace them because she had been home less than an hour when she'd gotten the call to get to Comanche Creek ASAP.

"I do own real boots," Livvy commented and wondered why she felt the need to defend herself.

With Reed's attention nailed to her, she lifted the lamp and immediately spotted the spatter on the dark wood. Without the light, it wasn't even detectable. There wasn't much, less than a dozen tiny drops, but it was consistent with a high-velocity impact.

"Shane's about my height," Reed continued. And he stood in the position that would have been the most likely spot to have produced that pattern.

It lined up.

Well, the droplets did anyway. She still had some doubts about Shane's story.

Livvy took her camera, slipped on a monochromatic lens and photographed the spatter. "Your deputy could have hit himself in the head. Not hard enough for him to lose consciousness. Just enough to give us the cast-off pattern we see here. Then, he could have hidden whatever he used to club himself."

Reed stared at her. "Or he could be telling the truth. If he is, that means we have a killer walking around scot-free."

Yes, and Livvy wasn't immune to the impact of that. It scratched away at old wounds, and even though she'd only been a Ranger for eighteen months, that was more than enough time for her to have learned that her baggage and old wounds couldn't be part of her job. She couldn't go back twenty years and right an old wrong.

Though she kept trying.

Livvy met Reed's gaze. It wasn't hard to do since he was still staring holes in her. "You really believe your deputy is incapable of killing his ex-lover?"

She expected an immediate answer. A *damn right* or some other manly affirmation. But Reed paused. Or rather he hesitated. His hands went to his hips, and he tipped his eyes to the ceiling.

"What?" Livvy insisted.

Reed shook his head, and for a moment she didn't think he would answer. "Shane and Marcie had a stormy relationship. I won't deny that. And since you'll find this out anyway, I had to suspend him once for excessive force when he was making an arrest during a domestic dispute. Still…I can't believe he'd commit a premeditated murder and set himself up."

Yes, that was a big question mark in her mind. If Shane had enough forensic training to set up someone, then why hadn't he chosen anyone but himself? That meant she was either dealing with an innocent man or someone who was very clever, and therefore very dangerous.

Because she was in such deep thought, Livvy jumped when a sound shot through the room. But it wasn't a threat. It was Reed's cell phone.

"Kirby," he said when he answered it.

That got her attention. Kirby Spears was the young deputy who'd assisted her on the scene and had carried the footprint castings back to the sheriff's office so a Ranger courier could pick them up and take them to the crime lab in Austin.

While she took a sample of one of the spatter droplets, Livvy listened to the conversation. Or rather that was what she tried to do. Hard to figure out what was going on with Reed's monosyllabic responses. However, his jaw muscles stirred again, and she thought she detected some frustration in those already intense eyes.

She bagged the blood-spatter sample, labeled it and put it in her equipment bag.

"Anything wrong?" Livvy asked the moment Reed ended the call.

"Maybe. While he was in town and running the investigating, Lieutenant Wyatt Colter made notes about the shoe sizes of the folks who live around here. He left the info at the station."

That didn't surprise Livvy. Lieutenant Colter was a thorough man. "And?"

"Kirby compared the size of the castings, and it looks as if three people could be a match. Of course, the prints could also have also been made by someone Marcie met during her two years on the run. The person might not even be from Comanche Creek."

Livvy couldn't help it. She huffed. "Other than you, who are two possible matches?"

"Jerry Collier, the head of the land office. He was also Marcie's former boss."

She had his bio, and it was one of the ones that Reed had picked from the file as a person who might be prone to breaking into the cabin. Later, she'd look into his possible motive for stealing a phone. "And the other potential match?"

Reed's jaw muscles did more than stir. They went iron-hard. "The mayor, Woody Sadler."

"Of course."

She groaned because she shouldn't have allowed Reed to stop her from arresting him. Or at least thoroughly searching him. Mayor Woody Sadler could have hidden that phone somewhere on his body and literally walked away with crucial evidence. Lost evidence that would get her butt in very hot water with her boss.

"I'll talk to him," Reed said.

"No. *I'll* talk to him." And this time she didn't intend to treat him like a mayor but a murder suspect.

In Reed's eyes, she saw the argument they were about to have. Livvy was ready to launch into the inevitable disagreement when she heard another sound. Not a cell phone this time.

Something crashed hard and loud against the cabin door.

Chapter Three

Reed drew his Smith and Wesson. Beside him, Livvy tossed the UV lamp and her glasses onto the sofa so she could do the same. Reed had already had his fill of unexpected guests today, and this sure as hell better not be somebody else trying to "help" Shane.

"Anyone out there?" Reed called out.

Nothing.

Since it was possible their visitor was Marcie's killer who'd returned to the scene of the crime, Reed approached the door with caution, and he kept away from the windows so he wouldn't be ambushed. He tried to put himself between Livvy and the door. It was an automatic response, one he would have done for anyone. However, she apparently didn't appreciate it because she maneuvered herself to his side again.

Reed reached for the doorknob, but stopped.

"Smoke?" he said under his breath. A moment later, he confirmed that was exactly what it was. If there was a fire out there, he didn't want to open the door and have the flames burst at them.

There was another crashing sound. This time it came

from the rear of the cabin. Livvy turned and aimed her gun in that direction. Reed kept his attention on the front of the place.

Hell.

What was happening? Was someone trying to break in? Or worse. Was someone trying to kill them?

In case it was the *or worse,* Reed knew he couldn't wait any longer. He peered out from the side of the window.

And saw something he didn't want to see.

"Fire!" he relayed to Livvy.

She raced to the back door of the cabin. "There's a fire here, too."

A dozen scenarios went through his mind, none of them good. He grabbed his phone and pressed the emergency number for the fire department.

"See anyone out there?" Reed asked, just as soon as he requested assistance.

"No. Do you?"

"No one," Reed confirmed. "Just smoke." And lots of it. In fact, there was already so much black billowy smoke that Reed couldn't be sure there was indeed a fire to go along with it. Still, he couldn't risk staying put. "We have to get out of here now."

Livvy took that as gospel because she hurried to the table, grabbed the files and the other evidence she'd gathered and shoved all of it and her other supplies into her equipment bag. She hoisted the bag over her shoulder, freeing her hand so she could use her gun. Unfortunately, it was necessary because Reed might need her as backup.

"Watch the doors," he insisted.

Not that anyone was likely to come through them with the smoke and possible fires, but he couldn't take that chance. They were literally under siege right now and anything was possible. The smoke was already pouring through the windows and doors, and it wouldn't be long before the cabin was completely engulfed.

The cabin wasn't big by anyone's standards. There was a basic living, eating and cooking area in the main room. One bedroom and one tiny bath were on the other side of the cabin. There was no window in the bathroom so he went to the lone one in the bedroom. He looked out, trying to stay out of any potential kill zone for a gunman, and he saw there was no sign of fire here. Thank God. Plus, it was only a few yards from a cluster of trees Livvy and he could use for cover.

"We can get out this way," Reed shouted. The smoke was thicker now. Too thick. And it cut his breath. It must have done the same for Livvy because he heard her cough.

He unlocked the window, shoved it up and pushed out the screen. The fresh air helped him catch his breath, but he knew the outside of the cabin could be just as dangerous as the inside.

"Anyone out there?" Livvy asked.

"I don't see anyone, but be ready just in case."

The person who'd thrown the accelerant or whatever might have used it as a ruse to draw them out. It was entirely possible that someone would try to kill them the moment they climbed out. Still, there was no choice here. Even though he'd already called the fire department, it would take them twenty minutes or more to respond to this remote area.

If they stayed put, Livvy and he could be dead by then.

"I'll go first," he instructed. He took her equipment bag and hooked it over his shoulder. That would free her up to run faster. "Cover me while I get to those trees."

She nodded. Coughed. She was pale, Reed noticed, but she wasn't panicking. Good. Because they both needed a clear head for this.

Reed didn't waste any more time. With his gun as aimed and ready as it could be, he hoisted himself over the sill and climbed out. He started running the second his feet touched the ground.

"Now," he told Livvy. He dropped the equipment bag and took cover behind the trees. Aimed. And tried to spot a potential gunman who might be on the verge of ambushing them.

Livvy snaked her body through the window and raced toward him. Despite the short distance, she was breathing hard by the time she reached him. She turned, putting her back to his. Good move, because this way they could cover most of the potential angles for an attack.

But Reed still didn't see anyone.

He blamed that on the smoke. It was a thick cloud around the cabin now. There were fires, both on the front porch and the back, and scattered around the fires were chunks of what appeared to be broken glass. The flames weren't high yet, but it wouldn't take them long to eat their way through the all-wood structure. And any potential evidence inside would be destroyed right along with it. If this arsonist was out to help Shane, then he was sadly mistaken.

Of course, the other possibility was that the real killer had done this.

It would be the perfect way to erase any traces of himself. Well, almost any traces. There was some potential evidence in Livvy's equipment bag. Maybe the person responsible wouldn't try to come after it.

But he rethought that.

A showdown would bring this fire-setting bozo out into the open, and Reed would be able to deal with him.

"Will the fire department make it in time to save the cabin?" Livvy asked between short bursts of air.

"No." And as proof of that, the flames shots up, engulfing the front door and swooshing their way to the cedar-shake roof. The place would soon be nothing but cinders and ash.

Reed was about to tell her that they'd have to stay put and watch the place burn since there was no outside hose to even attempt to put a dent in the flames. But he felt Livvy tense. It wasn't hard to feel because her back was right against his.

"What's wrong?" Reed whispered.

"I think I see someone."

Reed shifted and followed her gaze. She was looking in the direction of the county road, which was just down the hill from the cabin. Specifically, she was focused on the path that Woody had taken earlier. He didn't see anyone on the path or road, so he tried to pick through the woods and the underbrush to see what had alerted Livvy.

Still nothing.

"Look by my SUV," she instructed.

The vehicle was white and barely visible from his angle so Reed repositioned himself and looked down the slope. At first, nothing.

Then, something.

There was a flash of movement at the rear of her vehicle, but with just a glimpse he couldn't tell if it was animal or human.

"There's evidence in the SUV," she said. Her breathing was more level now, but that statement was loaded with fear and tension. "I'd photographed the cabin and exterior with a highly sensitive digital camera. Both it and the photo memory card are inside in a climate controlled case, along with some possible hair and fibers that I gathered from the sofa with a tape swatch."

Oh, hell. All those items could be critical to this investigation.

"The SUV's locked," she added.

For all the good that'd do. After all, the person out there had been gutsy enough to throw Molotov cocktails at the cabin with both Reed and a Texas Ranger inside, and he could have broken the lock on the SUV or bashed in a window.

Livvy grabbed her equipment bag from the ground and repositioned her gun. Reed knew what she had in mind, and he couldn't stop her from going to her vehicle to check on the evidence. But what he could do was assist.

"Stay close to the treeline," he instructed.

He stepped to her side so that she would be semi-sheltered from the open path. Another automatic response. But this time, Livvy didn't object. However, what she did do was move a lot faster than he'd anticipated.

Reed kept up with her while he tried to keep an eye on their surroundings and her SUV. None of the doors or windows appeared to be open, but he wouldn't be surprised if it'd been burglarized. Obviously, someone didn't want them to process that evidence.

He saw more movement near the SUV. A shadow, maybe. Or maybe someone lurking just on the other side near the rear bumper. Behind them, the fire continued to crackle and burn, and there was a crash when the roof of the cabin gave way and plummeted to the ground. Sparks and ashes scattered everywhere, some of them making their way to Livvy and him.

Livvy didn't stop. She didn't look back. But when Reed saw more movement, he latched on to her arm and pulled her behind an oak. This was definitely a situation where it would do no good to try to sneak up on the perp because the perp obviously was better positioned. Despite the cover of the trees, Livvy and he were in a vulnerable situation.

"This is Sheriff Hardin," he called out. "Get your hands in the air so I can see them."

He hadn't expected the person to blindly obey. And he didn't. Reed caught a glimpse of someone wearing a dark blue baseball cap.

Reed shifted his gun. Took aim—just as there was a crashing sound, followed by a flash of light. Someone had broken the SUV window and thrown another Molotov cocktail into the vehicle.

"He set the SUV on fire," Livvy said, bolting out from cover.

Reed pulled her right back. "He might have a gun." Except there was no *might* in this. The guy was probably armed and dangerous, and he couldn't have Livvy running right into an ambush.

"But the evidence…" she protested.

Yeah. That was a huge loss. Like Livvy, his instincts were to race down there and try to save what he could, but to do that might be suicide.

"He could want you dead," Reed warned.

That stopped Livvy from struggling. "Because of the evidence I gathered from the cabin?"

Reed nodded and waited for the rest of that to sink in. It didn't take long.

"Shane couldn't have done this," she concluded.

"No." Reed kept watch on the vehicle and the area in case the attacker doubled back toward them or tried to escape.

"But someone who wanted to exonerate him could have," Livvy added.

Reed nodded again. "That means the fire starter must have thought you saw or found something in the cabin that would be crucial evidence."

That also meant Livvy was in danger.

Reed cursed. This was turning into a tangled mess, and he already had too much to do without adding protecting Livvy to the list.

In the distance Reed heard the siren from the fire department. Soon, they'd be there. He glanced at the cabin. Then at Livvy's SUV. There wouldn't be much to save, but if he could catch the person responsible he might get enough answers to make up for the evidence they'd lost.

More movement. Reed spotted the baseball cap again. The guy was crouched down, and the cap created a shadow that hid his face. He couldn't even tell if it was a man or a woman. But whoever it was, the person was getting away.

"Stay put," Reed told Livvy.

Now it was her turn to catch onto his arm. "Remember that part about him having a gun."

Reed remembered, but he had to try to find out who was behind this.

"Back me up," he told her. That was to get her to stay put, but the other reason was he didn't want this cap-wearing guy to sneak up on him. Reed wouldn't be able to hear footsteps or much else with the roar of the fire and the approaching siren.

Keeping low as well, Reed stepped out from the meager cover of the oak. He kept his gun ready and aimed, and he started to run.

So did the other guy.

Using the smoke as cover, the culprit darted through the woods on the other side of the SUV and raced through the maze of trees. If Reed didn't catch up with him soon, it'd be too late. He ran down the hill, cursing the uneven clay-mix dirt that was slick in spots. Somehow, he made it to the bottom without falling and breaking his neck.

Reed didn't waste any time trying to save the SUV. The inside was already engulfed in flames. Instead, he sprinted past it, but Reed only made it a few steps before there was another sound.

Behind him, the SUV exploded.

He dodged the fiery debris falling all around him and sprinted after the person who'd just come close to killing them.

Chapter Four

Livvy dove to the ground and used the tree to shelter herself from the burning SUV parts that spewed through the air. She waited, listening, but it was impossible to hear anything, especially Reed. Beyond the black smoke cloud on the far side of what was left of her vehicle, she saw him sprint into the woods.

Since Reed might need backup, she got up, grabbed the equipment bag and went after him. Livvy kept to the trees that lined the path and then gave the flaming SUV a wide berth in case there was a secondary explosion. She'd barely cleared the debris when the fire engine screamed to a stop on the two-lane road.

"Sergeant Hutton," she said, identifying herself to the men who barreled from the engine. "Sheriff Hardin and I are in pursuit of a suspect."

Livvy hurried after Reed but was barely a minute into her trek when she saw Reed making his way back toward her. Not walking. Running.

"What's wrong?" she asked.

Reed drew in a hard breath. "I couldn't find him, and I was afraid he would double back and come after you."

Because the adrenaline was pumping through her and her heart was pounding in her ears, it took Livvy a moment to realize what he'd said. "I'm a Texas Ranger," she reminded him. "If he'd doubled back, I could have taken care of myself."

Reed tossed her a glance and started toward the fire department crew. "I didn't want him to shoot you and then steal the evidence bag," he clarified.

Oh. So, maybe it wasn't a me-Tarzan response after all. And once again, Livvy felt as if she'd been trumped when she was the one in charge.

By God, this was her case and her crime scene.

She followed Reed back to the chaos. The fire department already had their hose going, but there was nothing left to save. Worse, with everyone racing around the SUV and the cabin, it would be impossible to try to determine which footprints had been left by the perpetrator.

Reed stopped in front of a fifty-something Hispanic man, and they had a brief conversation that Livvy couldn't hear. A minute later, Reed rejoined her.

"Come on," he said. "We'll use my truck to take that evidence to my office."

Livvy looked around and realized there was nothing she could do here, so she followed Reed past the cabin to a back trail. It wasn't exactly a relaxing stroll because both Reed and she hurried and kept their weapons ready. With good reason, too. Someone had just destroyed crucial evidence, and that same someone might come after them. The woods were thick and ripe territory for an ambush.

Reed unlocked his black F-150 and they climbed in

and sped away. He immediately got on the phone to his deputy, and while Reed filled in Deputy Spears, Livvy knew she had to contact her boss, Lieutenant Wyatt Colter.

She grabbed her cell, took a deep breath and made the call. Since there was no way to soften it, she just spilled it and told him all about the burned cabin, her SUV and the destroyed evidence.

On the other end of the line, Lieutnenant Colter cursed. "You didn't have the evidence secured?"

"I did, in the locked SUV, but the perp set it on fire." She was thankful that she'd already stashed her personal items at the Bluebonnet Inn where she'd be staying so at least she would have a change of clothes and her toiletries. Of course, she would have gladly exchanged those items, along with every penny in her bank account, if she could get back that evidence.

More cursing from the lieutenant, and she heard him relay the information to someone else who was obviously in the room with him. Great. Now, everyone at the regional office would know about this debacle.

"Things are crazy here," Lieutenant Colter explained. "I'm tracking down those illegally sold Native American artifacts, and I'm at a critical point in negotiations. But I'll be out there by early afternoon."

"No!" Livvy couldn't get that out fast enough. "There's no need, and there's nothing you can do. I have everything under control."

The lieutenant's long hesitation let her know he wasn't buying that. "I'll talk with the captain and get back to you."

"I don't need reinforcements," she added, but Livvy

was talking to herself because Lieutenant Colter had already hung up on her.

"Problem?" Reed asked the moment she ended the call.

"No," she lied.

He made a sound to indicate he knew it was a lie.

Since it was a whopper, Livvy tried to hurry past the subject. "After I get this evidence logged in and started, I'd like to question Shane about the murder."

Reed didn't answer right away. He had her wait several moments, making Livvy wish she'd made it sound more like an order and not a request.

"Shane will cooperate," Reed finally said. He paused again. "And while you're talking to him, I'll call your lieutenant and let him know this wasn't your fault."

"Don't." She stared at him as he drove onto the highway that led to town. "I don't need your help." Though she probably did. Still, Livvy wouldn't allow Reed to defend her when she was capable of doing it herself. "I'll call him in an hour or two and explain there's no need for him to be here."

And somehow, she would have to make him understand.

"This case seems personal to you," Reed commented. "Why? Did you know Marcie?"

"No." But he was right. This was personal. Murders always were. "My mother was murdered when I was six, and she was about the same age as Marcie. This brings back…memories."

And she had no idea why she'd just admitted that. Sheez. The chaos had caused her to go all chatty.

"Was the killer caught?" Reed asked.

Livvy groaned softly. She hadn't meant for this to turn into a conversation. "No. He escaped to Mexico and has never been found."

"That explains why you're wrapped so tight."

She blinked. Frowned. "Excuse me?"

"You think if you solve Marcie's murder, then in a small way, you'll get justice for your mom."

She was sure her mouth dropped open when she scowled at him. "What—did you take Psych 101 classes along with those forensic workshops?"

He shook his head. "Personal experience. My dad was shot and killed when I was a kid. Every case turns out to be about him." Reed lifted his shoulder. "Can't help it. It's just an old wound that can't be healed."

Yes.

Livvy totally understood that.

"That's why I jumped to defend Woody back there," Reed continued. "He raised me. He became the dad who was taken away from me." But then he paused. "That doesn't mean I can't be objective. I can be."

She wanted to grumble a *hmmmp* to let him know she had her doubts about that objectivity, but her doubts weren't as strong as they had been an hour earlier. Livvy blamed that on their escape from death together. That created a special camaraderie. So did their tragic pasts. For that matter so did this bizarre attraction she felt for him. All in all, it led to a union that she didn't want or need.

"Oh, man," Reed groaned.

Livvy looked ahead at the two-story white limestone building with a triple-arch front and reinforced glass doors. It was the sheriff's office, among other things.

Livvy had learned from Deputy Spears that it also housed the jail and several municipal offices.

Right next to the sheriff's building was an identical structure for the mayor's office and courthouse. However, it wasn't the weathered facades of the buildings that had likely caused Reed's groan. As he brought the truck to a stop, he had his attention fastened to the two men and a Native American woman standing on the steps. Another attractive woman with long red hair was sitting in a car nearby.

"Trouble?" Livvy asked.

"Maybe. Not from the redhead. She's Jessie Becker, but her father's the one on the right. He's probably here to stir up some trouble."

Jonah was the owner of the cabin. And, as far as Livvy was concerned, he was a prime murder suspect. Even if he hadn't been the one to actually kill Marcie, he might have information about it.

Though she'd scoured Jonah's bio, this was Livvy's first look at the man, and he certainly lived up to his reputation of being intimating and hard-nosed. Jonah might have been wearing a traditional good-guy white cowboy hat, but the stare he gave her was all steel and ice.

"You let somebody burn down my cabin," Jonah accused the moment Reed and she stepped from the truck. "The fire chief just called. Said it was a total loss."

"We didn't exactly *let* it happen," Reed snarled. He stopped. Met Jonah eye-to-eye. "There was a phone stolen from the cabin before the place was set on fire. Know anything about that?"

Jonah's mouth tightened. "Now, you're accusing me of thievery from a place I own?"

"I'm asking, not accusing," Reed clarified, though from his tone, it could have been either. "But I want an answer."

The demand caused a standoff with the two men staring at each other. "I didn't take anything from the cabin," Jonah finally said, "because I haven't been out there. Last I heard, you'd roped off the place and said for everybody to stay away. So, I stayed away," he added with a touch of smugness.

If Reed believed him, he didn't acknowledge it.

"I'm Billy Whitley," the other man greeted Livvy, extending his hand to her. He tipped his head to the Native American woman beside him. "And this is my wife, Charla."

Livvy shifted her equipment bag and shook hands with both of them. "Sergeant Hutton."

Unlike Jonah, Billy wasn't wearing a cowboy hat, and the khaki-wearing man sported a smile that seemed surprisingly genuine. "Welcome to Comanche Creek, Sergeant Hutton."

"Yes, welcome," Charla repeated, though it wasn't as warm a greeting as her husband's had been. And she didn't just look at Livvy—the woman's intense coffee-brown eyes stared.

Livvy didn't offer her first name, as Billy had done to her. Yes, it was silly, but she wanted to hang on to every thread of authority she had left. After what'd just happened, that wasn't much, but somehow she had to establish that she was the one in charge here. That wasn't easy to do with Reed storming past Jonah and Billy.

And her.

That left her trailing along after him.

"I'm the county clerk here," Billy continued. "Charla is an administrative assistant for the mayor." All three followed into the building, too. "I handle the records and such, and if I can help you in any way, just let me know."

That *such* might become important to Livvy since Billy would be in charge of deeds, and the land that Jonah had bought might play into what was happening now. Of course, Livvy had a dozen other things to do before digging into what might have been an illegal land deal.

Jonah caught up with them and fell in step to her left. Since the entry hall was massive, at least fifteen feet wide, it wasn't hard for the four to walk side by side, especially with Reed ahead of them. "I'm not even gonna get an apology for my cabin?" Jonah complained.

"I'm sorry," Livvy mumbled, and she was sincere. Losing the cabin and the evidence inside was a hard blow to the case.

Reed turned into a room about midway down the hall, and he walked past a perky-looking auburn-haired receptionist who stood and then almost immediately sat back down to take an incoming call.

They walked by a room where Deputy Spears was on the phone as well, but he called out to her, "The castings are on the way to the lab. The courier just picked them up."

"Thanks," Livvy managed but didn't stop.

She continued to follow the fast-walking Reed into his office. Like the man, it was a bit of a surprise. His desk was neat, organized, and the slim computer monitor and equipment made it look more modern than Livvy had thought it would be. There was a huge calendar on the wall, and it was filled with appointments at precise times, measured not in hours but in quarter hours.

"You can put the equipment bag there," Reed instructed, pointing to a table pushed against one of the walls. There was also an evidence locker nearby. Good. She wanted to secure the few items she had left.

Reed snatched up the phone. "I need to call some of the other sheriffs in the area and have them send over deputies to scour the woods for anything the arsonist might have left behind. After that, I'll take you up to the jail so you can talk to Shane."

Reed proceeded to make that call, but he also shot a what-are-you-still-doing-here? glare at Billy, Charla and Jonah, who were hovering in the narrow doorway and watching Livvy's every move. Livvy didn't think it was her imagination that all three were extremely interested in what she had in the equipment bag. Still, Billy tipped two fingers to his forehead in a mock salute and Charla and he left.

Jonah didn't.

"So, did you come to town to arrest me for Marcie's murder?" Jonah asked her.

Livvy spared him a glance and plopped her bag onto the table. "Why, are you confessing to it?"

"Careful," Jonah warned, and his tone was so chilling that it prompted Livvy to look at him.

"I'm always careful. And thorough," she threatened back. She tried not to let her suspicions of this man grow. After all, they had a suspect in jail, but she wondered if Shane had acted alone.

Or if he'd acted at all.

It wouldn't be a pleasant task to challenge Shane's guilt or innocence because if she proved Shane hadn't murdered Marcie, then she would have to prove that someone else had. That was certain to rile a lot of people.

She remembered the uncomfortable stare that Charla Whitley had given her. And the way the mayor had reminded her of Reed's authority. She wasn't winning any Miss Congeniality contests—and probably wouldn't.

"Good day, Mr. Becker," Livvy said, dismissing Jonah, and she took out the bag with the sample from the blood spatter. If this was indeed Shane's blood, and if future analysis of the pattern indicated that it was real castoff from blunt force, then that would put some doubt in her mind.

Since Reed was still on the phone, Livvy secured her bag in the evidence locker, and with the blood sample clutched in her hand, she walked to the doorway. Jonah was still there, but she merely stepped around him and went to Deputy Spears's office. She shut the door so they'd have some privacy.

"I need this analyzed ASAP," she instructed. "It's possible that it's Shane's blood."

Kirby Spears nodded. "I can run it over to the coroner. He does a lot of this type of work for us, and we have Shane's DNA on file in the computer so we can compare the sample." He took the bag and put his initials on the chain of custody form.

Again, Livvy was surprised with the efficiency. "What about the murder weapon and the bullet?"

"The bullet's still being analyzed at the Ranger crime lab, and there's no match to the gun. We have the serial number, but so far, there's no info in the database about it."

Livvy made a mental note to call the crime lab, but first she wanted to visit Shane. Without Reed. Even though Reed had said he would be the one to take her, she didn't need or want his help during this particular interrogation. She knew how to question a suspect.

"Where's the jail?" she asked the deputy.

"Up the stairs, to the right."

Livvy thanked him and walked back into the hall. She halfway expected Jonah to be waiting there, but saw thankfully he had left. Since Reed was still on the phone, she made her way up the stairs to where she found a guard sitting at a desk. He wore a uniform from a civilian security agency, and he obviously knew who she was because he stood.

"Shane's this way," he commented and led her down the short hall flanked on each side with cells. All were empty except for the last one. There, she found the deputy lying on the military-style cot.

Livvy's first thought was that he didn't look like a killer. With his dark hair and piercing blue eyes, he looked more like a grad student. A troubled one, though.

"Sergeant Hutton," he said, slowly getting to his feet.

"Word travels fast," she mumbled.

The corner of his mouth lifted into a half smile that didn't quite make it to his eyes. "There aren't many secrets in Comanche Creek. Well, except for the secret of who murdered Marcie. I loved her." He shook his head. "I wouldn't have killed her."

"The evidence says differently."

He walked closer and curved his fingers around the

thick metal bars. "But since I didn't do it, there must be evidence to prove that. Promise me that you'll dig for the truth. Don't let anyone, including Jonah, bully you."

She shrugged. "Why would Jonah want to bully me?"

"Because you're a woman. An outsider, at that. He won't respect your authority. For that matter, most won't, and that includes the mayor."

Well, Livvy would have to change their minds.

"What do you know about a cell phone that I found in the ashes of the fireplace?" she asked.

There was a flash of surprise in his eyes. Then, another headshake. "I don't know. Is it Marcie's?"

"Maybe. Any reason the mayor would steal the phone to try to help you out?"

"Woody? Not a chance. He might not care for outsiders like you, but he wouldn't break the law. Why? You think he had something to do with the fire at the cabin?"

Livvy jumped right on that. "How'd you know about it?"

"The guard. His best friend runs the fire department."

"Cozy," Livvy mumbled. But she didn't add more because she heard the footsteps. She glanced up the hall and saw Reed making his way toward them.

"You could have waited," Reed mumbled.

Livvy squared her shoulders. "There was no reason. I'm trying to organize my case, and questioning Deputy Tolbert is a critical part of that."

Reed gave her a disapproving glance—she was getting used to those—before he looked at Shane. "We found blood spatter on the mantel in the cabin." It definitely wasn't the voice of a lawman, but it wasn't exactly friendly, either.

Shane blew out his breath as if relieved. "I've been going over and over what happened, and I'm pretty sure the person who clubbed me was a man. Probably close to my height because I didn't get a sense of anyone looming behind me before I was hit. I think you're also looking for someone who might be left-handed because the blow came from my left."

"Did you notice any particular smell or sound?" Livvy asked at the same moment Reed asked, "Did you remember what he used to hit you?"

Reed and she looked at each other.

Frowned.

"No smell or sound," Shane answered. "And I saw the object out of the corner of my eye. I think it might have been a baseball bat."

Livvy was about to ask if the bat had possibly been in or around the cabin, but her phone rang. One glance at the caller ID, and she knew it was a call she had to take—her boss, Lieutnenant Colter. She stepped away from the cell and walked back toward the desk area. Behind her, she heard Reed continue to talk to Shane.

"Livvy," Lieutenant Colter greeted her. "I wanted to let you know that I won't be able to get to Comanche Creek after all. There's too much going on here. And with a suspect already arrested—"

"Don't worry. I can handle things."

His pause was long and unnerving. "I talked with the captain, and we've agreed to give you three days to process the scene and the evidence. By then, we can send in another Ranger. One with more experience."

Oh, that last bit stung.

"Three days," Livvy said under her breath. Not much time, but enough. She would use those three days to prove herself and determine if the evidence did indeed conclude that the deputy had murdered his former girl-friend. "Thank you for this opportunity."

"Don't thank me yet. Livvy, there's one condition about you staying there."

Everything inside her went still. "What?"

"You're not in charge of this case. Sheriff Reed Hardin is. And while you're there in Comanche Creek, you'll be taking your orders from him."

Chapter Five

Reed made his way across the back parking lot of the sheriff's building. With the sun close to setting, the sky was a dark iron-gray, and the drizzle was picking up speed. He hadn't even bothered to grab an umbrella from the basket next to his desk, but then he hadn't thought Livvy would creep along at a snail's pace either.

"This isn't necessary," Livvy complained again. She was a good ten feet behind him, and she had her equipment bag slung over her shoulder. "I can walk to the Bluebonnet Inn on my own."

Reed ignored her complaint and opened his truck door so she could climb inside. "The inn's a mile away, and in case you hadn't noticed, it's raining." And because her expression indicated she was still opposed to a lift, he added, "The sooner you get settled into your room, the sooner you can go over the recording of my initial interview with Shane."

Since Livvy had the envelope with the disk tucked under her arm, Reed knew she was anxious to get to it. But then, she was also anxious to be away from him, and a ride, even a short one, would only remind her that she'd essentially been demoted as lead on this case.

And he was in charge.

Reed didn't know who was more ticked off about that—Livvy or him. Even though he'd wanted to handle this investigation himself, he certainly hadn't asked to play boss to a Texas Ranger who already thought he was lower than hoof grit.

When Livvy stopped and stared at him, Reed huffed, blinked away the raindrops spattering on his eyelashes and got into his truck, leaving the passenger's-side door open. The rain had caused wisps of her hair to cling to her face and neck. No more sleek ponytail. The rain had also done something to her white shirt.

Something that Reed wished he hadn't noticed.

The fabric had become somewhat transparent and now clung to her bra and breasts. And the rest of her.

You're her temporary boss, he reminded himself.

But the reminder did zero good. Nada. Zip. His male brain and body were very attentive to Livvy's ample curves and that barely-there white lace bra she was wearing.

As if she'd realized where his attention was, her gaze dropped down to her chest. "Oh!" leaped from her mouth. And she slapped the large manila envelope over the now-transparent shirt. She also got in the truck. Fast. And slammed the door.

"You could have said something," she mumbled, strapping on her seat belt as if it were the enemy.

"I could have," he admitted, "but let's just say I was dumbfounded and leave it at that."

He drove away with her still staring at him, and her mouth was slightly open, too.

Reed didn't want to defend himself, especially since gawking at her had been a dumb thing to do, but her continuing stare prompted him to say something. "Hey, just because I wear this badge doesn't mean I'm not a red-blooded male."

"Great." And that was all she said for several moments. "This won't be a problem."

"This?" Yeah, it was stupid to ask, but Reed couldn't stop himself.

"My breasts. Your male red blood."

Well, that put him in his place and meant the attraction was one-sided. His side, specifically. Good. That would make these next three days easier.

Parts of his body disagreed.

Reed stopped in front of the Bluebonnet Inn, a two-story Victorian guesthouse that sported a crisp white facade with double wraparound porches and a ton of windows. Livvy got out ahead of him and seemed surprised when he got out as well and followed her up the steps.

"I just want to check on a few things," he explained.

"Such as?"

"Security."

That stopped her hand in mid-reach for the cut-glass doorknob. She studied his eyes, and then her forehead bunched up. "You think the person who burned the cabin might come after me?"

"It's a possibility." Reed glanced at her equipment bag. "He might be after that."

"There's no evidence in it. The blood's being

analyzed, and I left the photos of the spatter pattern at your office in the secure locker." Then she quickly added, "But the arsonist doesn't know that."

Reed nodded and opened the door. He didn't want to feel uneasy about Livvy's ability to protect herself. After all, as she'd already informed him, she was a Texas Ranger, trained with a firearm. And he was reasonably sure his feelings had nothing to do with her being a woman and more to do with the fact there was someone obviously hell-bent on destroying any and everything that might have been left at the crime scene.

Someone he likely called a friend or a neighbor. Not exactly a comforting feeling.

"Reed," the landlady greeted him when he stepped inside. Like most of the townsfolk, he'd known Betty Alice Sadler all his life. She was Woody's sister and the owner of the Bluebonnet Inn and she had a smile that could compete with the sun.

"Betty Alice," Reed greeted her back. He tipped his head to Livvy. "You've met Sergeant Hutton?"

The woman aimed one of her winning smiles at Livvy. "For a second or two when she dropped her things off this morning. In and out, she was, before we hardly had time to say a word." The smile faded, however, when she glanced at the bulky-looking suitcase and garment bag in the corner. "One of those McAllister boys was supposed to help me out around here today, but he didn't show up."

Reed knew what Betty Alice didn't explain. The woman had a bad back, and all the guestrooms were upstairs. No elevator, either. Taking up the bags herself would have been next to impossible.

"I'll carry them up," Reed volunteered. "Has anyone dropped by today? Maybe someone who could have slipped into the rooms?"

Betty Alice pressed her left palm against her chest. "Lord have mercy, I don't think so. But you know I'm not always at this desk. When I'm in the kitchen or watching my soaps, it's hard to hear if somebody comes in."

Yes, he did know, and that meant he needed to do some further checking. "I'm sure everything's fine. It's just we had some more problems out by Jonah Becker's cabin, and I want to take some precautions."

Betty Alice's hand slipped from her chest, and her chin came up a fraction. "Nobody around here would try to set fire to my place. Now, Jonah's cabin—well, that's a different story. Most folks know he's got money and things to burn so that cabin was no real loss to him. Still, I'm real sorry about the sergeant's car."

"How did you know about my car?" Livvy asked.

"My second cousin's a fireman, and he was at home when he got the call to respond. His wife heard what was going on and phoned me. I hope your car was insured."

"It was," Livvy assured her. And she walked toward her bags.

Reed walked toward them, too. "Let me guess—you put Sergeant Hutton in the pink room?" Reed asked Betty Alice.

The woman's smile returned. "I did. You know it's where I put all my single female guests. That room's my pride and joy. I hope you like it, Sergeant."

"I'm sure I will," Livvy answered, and in the same breath added, "I can carry the things myself."

He would have bet his paycheck that was what she was going to say, but Reed took the suitcase and garment bag anyway, and since Livvy had the equipment and the envelope, she couldn't exactly snatch the items away from him.

"You'll set the security alarm tonight?" Reed said to Betty Alice. "And lock all the windows and doors?"

"Of course. I'll keep my gun next to my bed, too. Since all that mess with Marcie, I'm being careful, just like you told me."

"Good. But I want you to be extra careful tonight, understand?"

Betty Alice bobbed her head and nibbled on her bottom lip that'd been dabbed liberally with dark red lipstick. Reed hated to worry the woman, but he wanted Livvy and her to be safe.

"I really can carry my own bags," Livvy repeated as they made their way up the stairs.

Reed stopped at the top of the stairs in front of the pink room and set down the bags. Yes, it was dangerous, but he turned and met Livvy eye-to-eye. Since she was only about four inches shorter than he was, that made things easier because he wanted lots of eye contact while he cleared the air.

"Three days is a long time for us to be at odds. Yeah, I know you can carry bags. I know you can protect yourself, but I'm an old-fashioned kind of guy. A cowboy. And it's not in my genes to stand back when I can do something to help. Now, if that insults you, I'm sorry. And I'm sorry in advance because I'm about to go in your room and make sure it's safe. Just consider that part of my supervisory duties, okay?"

The staring match started. Continued. Reed had been right about the eye contact. And the other close contact. After all, Livvy was still wearing that transparent blouse, and she smelled like the smoky bacon cheeseburger and chocolate malt the café had delivered not long before Reed and she had called it a night and left the office. Normally, Reed wouldn't have considered a burger and malt to be tempting scents, but they were working tonight.

"Okay," she said, her voice all silk and breath.

Or maybe the silk part was his imagination.

Nope. When she cleared her throat and repeated it, Reed realized this close contact was having an effect on her as well.

Both of them stepped back at the same time.

"I want to go back out to the cabin in the morning." She cleared her throat again. "Will you be able to arrange a vehicle for me?"

Reed mentally cleared his own throat and mind. "I can take you. Two of the nearby sheriffs sent deputies out to scour the woods. Don't worry, they all have forensic training. They won't contaminate the scene, and they might be able to find and secure any evidence before the rain washes it all away."

That was a Texas-size *might* though since it'd been drizzling most of the afternoon.

She turned toward the door. Stopped. Turned back. "I'm sorry."

Puzzled, Reed shook his head. "For what?"

"For being so…unfriendly. I'm just disappointed, that's all."

He didn't know which one of them looked more uncomfortable with that admission. "I understand. I didn't ask Lieutenant Colter to be in charge."

"I know. He doesn't trust me."

Reed shrugged. "Or maybe he just wanted you to have some help on a very tough investigation."

She made a sound to indicate she didn't agree with that and opened the door. He supposed the room had some charm with its lacy bedspread and delicate—aka prissy—Victorian furniture, but it was hard to see the charm when the entire room looked as if it'd been doused in Pepto-Bismol.

"It *really* is pink, isn't it?" Livvy mumbled.

"Yeah. You could ask for a different room, but trust me, you don't want to do that because then you'd have to listen to Betty Alice explain every décor decision that went into the final result."

"This'll be fine. After all, it's where she puts all her single female guests."

And that was one of the primary reasons Reed had wanted to accompany her to the room. Everyone in town would know Livvy was staying there. It wouldn't help to put her in a different room either because secrets had a very short shelf life in Comanche Creek.

Reed set down the bags and went to the adjoining bathroom to make sure it was empty. It was. No one was lurking behind the frilly shower curtain ready to start another fire. No threatening messages had been scrawled on the oval beveled mirror.

Maybe, just maybe, the threat had ended with the destruction of the SUV and cabin.

Reed was in such deep thought with this suite examination that it took him a moment to realize Livvy was standing in the bathroom door, and she was staring at him. "You're really concerned that I can't take care of myself. But I can. My specialty might be CSI, but my marksmanship skills are very good."

He didn't doubt her. Didn't doubt her shooting ability, either. But after the past few days, he wasn't sure any skill was good enough to stop what was happening.

"I have a spare bedroom at my place just on the edge of town," he offered. "And it's not pink," he added because he thought they both could use a little levity.

The corner of her mouth lifted. Not quite a smile though. And her eyes came to his. "Thanks but no thanks. I'll have a hard enough time getting people to respect me without them thinking that I'm sleeping with the boss."

He nodded. Paused. Reed walked past her and back into the bedroom. "They're likely to think that anyway."

Reed waited for her to look shocked. Or to protest it. But she didn't. "I take it you don't have a fiancée or long-time girlfriend?" she asked.

"No." And he left it at that.

Of course, Livvy would soon hear all about the breakup with Elena Carson four years ago when his high-school flame had decided to move to London to take a PR job. Heck, she'd even hear about the attorney from San Antonio that Reed had dated for a couple of months. The one who'd pressed him to marry her because her biological clock was ticking. And yeah, Livvy would even hear about the cocktail waitress who'd worn an eye-popping dress to the city hall Christmas party. No one would say he was a player, but he wouldn't be labeled a saint.

"What about Charla Whitley?" Livvy asked. "Did you date her?"

Reed was sure he was the one who looked a little shocked now. "No. What made you think that?"

"She was giving me the evil eye, and I thought it was maybe because of you. Probably had more to do with the fact that her husband could be a suspect, and she doesn't want me here investigating things."

Probably. But then, just about everyone in town was a suspect. Livvy could expect a lot of evil eyes in the next few days.

"What about you?" Reed asked, knowing it was a question that should be left unasked. "No fiancé or long-time boyfriend?"

She shook her head. "I don't have a lot of time for serious relationships."

"Ever?" And, of course, he should just hit himself so he'd stop prying, but for some stupid reason, a reason that had generated below his belt, he wanted to know more about Livvy Hutton.

"I dated someone in college, and it got serious. Well, on his part. You probably know it's hard to keep up with a personal life when the badge is there. And my badge is always there," she added, tapping the silver star on her chest while eyeing the one clipped to his belt.

He couldn't stop himself. "Must make for interesting sex if you never take off your badge."

There was another flash of surprise in her eyes. Then, she laughed. It was smoky and thick, the laugh of a woman who knew how to enjoy herself when the time was right. But she clamped off the laugh as quickly as she had the smile.

"You should go," she murmured. There it was

again. The sound of her voice trickled through him. Warm and silky.

Reed looked at her face. At her mouth. And knew Livvy was right. He should go. Betty Alice was probably already on the phone to her garden club, telling them that the sheriff had been in the lady Ranger's room for a whole ten minutes.

A lot could happen in ten minutes.

His imagination was a little too good at filling in the possibilities. Sex against the door. On the floor. Location wasn't important. It was the sex that he wanted.

But he wouldn't get it.

Reed forced himself to repeat that several times until it finally sank in.

"I'll pick you up at 7:00 a.m.," he told her. "And after a bite or two of breakfast at the café, we can drive out to the cabin."

"Can we get the breakfast to go?" she asked. "I'm anxious to return to the crime scene, and we can eat on the way."

Reed nodded. "Takeout, it is. I'll even see if the cook can figure out a way to add some chocolate to whatever's on the breakfast menu."

Livvy blinked. "How did you know I like chocolate?"

"Your breath, this morning. I smelled it. Milky Way?"

"Snickers," she confessed.

He didn't know why, but that confession seemed just as intimate as the sex thoughts he'd been having about her. He obviously needed to remember that he was a badass Texas sheriff. A surly one at that. Certainly not a man who cared to make a mental note to buy Livvy a Snickers bar or two.

"I'll see you in the morning." Reed headed out the door. However, he did wait in the hall until Livvy had closed it and he heard her engage the lock. She also moved something—a chair, from the sound of it—in front of the door.

Good.

Livvy was at least a little scared, and though that likely meant she wouldn't get much sleep, her vigilance might keep her safe. Now, Reed had to make sure that that safety extended to other things.

As soon as the borrowed deputies got to his office, he would send one of them out to patrol Main Street. Specifically, the Bluebonnet Inn. And he'd make copies of anything Livvy had left in the storage locker. That way, if the arsonist struck again, they wouldn't lose what little evidence they had left.

While Reed was making his mental list, he also added that he needed to call about the bullet, the missing cell phone, the gun and the DNA sample that Livvy had sent to the coroner.

It'd be another night short on sleep.

Reed went down the stairs, said goodnight to Betty Alice and watched as the woman double-locked the door and set the security alarm. Since the inn was also Betty Alice's home, it meant she, too, would be staying there, and Reed hoped everything would stay safe and secure. No more fires.

Because the drizzle had turned to a hard rain, he hurried down the steps toward his truck. But something had him stopping. He glanced around and spotted the black car parked just up the street in front of the newspaper office. That office had been closed for several hours, and there should have been no one parked there.

Reed tried to pick through the rain and the darkness and see if anyone was inside.

There was.

But because the windows were heavily tinted, he couldn't see the person. Nor the license plate. However, Reed could see the sticker that indicated it was a rental car. Definitely not a common sight in Comanche Creek.

He eased his hand over the butt of his Smith and Wesson and started toward the car. Maybe this had nothing to do with anything. Or maybe the fact it was a rental meant this was someone not local. Maybe someone Marcie had met while she was in hiding.

Either way, Reed braced himself for the worst.

The farther he made it down the sidewalk, the less he could see. That was because the only streetlights in this area were the two that flanked the front of the Bluebonnet Inn. The person had chosen the darkest spot to park.

And wait.

Reed was about fifteen feet away from the vehicle when he saw the movement inside. Someone gripped onto the wheel. A moment later, the engine roared to life. Reed kept moving toward it, but the sudden lurching motion of the car had him stopping in his tracks.

It happened in a split second. There was more movement from the driver, and the car barreled forward.

Right at Reed.

Drawing his gun, he dove to the side. And not a moment too soon. He landed on the wet grass of the vacant lot, his shoulder ramming into a chunk of limestone.

The car careened right into the spot where seconds earlier he'd been standing.

Reed cursed and came up on one knee. Ready to fire. Or to dive out of the way if the car came at him again.

But it didn't.

The driver gunned the engine, and before he sped away, Reed caught just a glimpse of the person inside.

Hell.

Chapter Six

"Where the heck is he?" Livvy heard Reed demand.

He'd been making such demands from everyone he'd called, and this wasn't his first call. Reed had been on the phone the entire time since he'd picked her up at the Bluebonnet Inn ten minutes earlier. And while Livvy ate her scrambled-egg breakfast taco that Reed had brought her from the diner, she tried to make sense of what was going on.

"Leave him another message," Reed added, his voice as tense as the muscles of his face. "Tell him to call me the minute he gets back." And with that, Reed slapped his phone shut and shoved it into his pocket.

Livvy waited for an explanation of what had gotten him into such a foul mood, but he didn't say a word. She wondered if it was personal, and if so, she wanted to stay far away from it. There was already too much personal stuff going on between Reed and her, including that little chat they'd had about chocolate, badges and relationships.

She'd dreamed about him.

Not a tame dream either, but one that involved kissing and sex.

Hot, sweaty sex.

She would have preferred to dream about catching a killer or processing evidence, but instead she'd gotten too-vivid images of what it would be like to be taken by a man who almost certainly knew how to take.

Livvy felt herself blush. And decided she needed a change of thoughts. "Is there a problem?" she asked Reed.

Still no immediate answer, which confirmed there was indeed something wrong. "When I was leaving the Bluebonnet last night, I saw a rental car parked just up the street. When I went to check it out, the driver gunned the engine and nearly plowed right into me."

Oh, mercy. "Any reason you didn't tell me this sooner?"

More hesitation. "I wanted to check into a few things first."

Which, of course, explained nothing. Well, nothing other than why during the night there'd been a deputy positioned in a cruiser on the street directly in front of the inn. When Livvy had noticed him, she'd gotten upset with Reed because she'd assumed once again that he thought she couldn't take care of herself. But the rental-car incident was what had prompted him to add some extra security to the inn.

Reed had wanted someone in place in case the guy returned.

With her appetite gone now, Livvy wrapped up the rest of the breakfast taco and shoved it back into the bag. "Were you hurt?" she asked, starting with the most obvious question.

"No." That answer was certainly fast enough, though

she did notice the scrape on the back of his right hand. It was red and raw.

Livvy moved on to the next questions. "Any idea who the driver was, and why he'd want to do something like this?"

The possible theories started to fire through her head, but the one at the forefront was that the person who'd done this had also destroyed the cabin and her SUV. And this person wanted all the evidence destroyed and the investigation halted so the real killer wouldn't be caught. Or maybe the person thought the real killer was already behind bars and wanted him free.

Shane's father, maybe.

Or the other suspects.

Jerry Collier, Billy Whitley, Charla, Jonah Becker or Woody.

Reed stopped his truck just off the road that led to the burned-out cabin. Just yards away there was a police cruiser from another county. The vehicle no doubt belonged to the backups that Reed had called in. But it wasn't the activity that had her staring at him. Suddenly, the calls and his surly mood made sense.

"You saw the driver," she accused.

He scrubbed his hand over his face. "I saw his hat. A white Stetson with a rattler's tail on the band." Reed got out and slammed the door.

It didn't take her long to remember where she'd seen one matching that description. "Woody Sadler's hat," she clarified, getting out as well. Since Reed had already started to storm up the hill, she had to grab her equipment bag and hurry to keep up with him.

"A hat like his," Reed corrected.

"Or his," Livvy corrected back. She thought of the calls Reed had made in the truck. "And you haven't been able to speak to Woody to ask where he was last night."

The glance he gave her was hard and cold, but he didn't deny it. "Woody's secretary said he'd decided to take a last-minute fishing trip. His cell phone doesn't have service at the lake." He stopped so abruptly that Livvy nearly lost her balance trying to do the same. He aimed his index finger at her. "But let's get one thing straight. Woody wouldn't have tried to run me down."

Livvy wanted to argue with that, but it was true. It wouldn't make sense. Now, if Woody had come after her, that would have been more believable.

"Okay." Livvy nodded. "Then that means someone wanted you to think it was Woody. Who would have access to a hat like that?"

"Anyone in Texas," he grumbled.

Of course. It was dumb of her to ask. "But you're sure it was a man behind the wheel of the car?"

"Pretty sure. The person had the hat angled so that I couldn't see his face. And I got just a glimpse."

She glanced at the scrape on his hand again. Reed had gotten lucky, because even if this had been a stunt to scare them, it could have gone terribly wrong and he could have been killed. The thought made her a little sick to her stomach.

Okay, not sick sick.

Troubled sick.

She didn't like to think of anything bad happening to him, even though they were, for all practical purposes, still on opposite sides of a very tall fence.

"What?" he asked, glancing down at his hand and then at her.

"Nothing." And so that it would stay that way, she started up the hill again.

Reed snagged her by the arm and stopped her in her tracks. *"Something,"* he corrected.

She thought of her dream, felt the blush return. Livvy tried to shrug, and she quickly tried to get her mind off those raunchy images. "I know you're the boss, but from now on, please don't keep anything from me that might relate to the case."

And to make sure this didn't continue, she pulled away from his grip and started toward the uniformed deputy standing near the burned-out swatch of her SUV. Someone had already gathered up the debris. Nearby, just several feet inside the start of the thick brush and trees, she spotted a uniformed officer.

Livvy also spotted the soggy, muddy ground that was caking onto her boots. That mud wasn't good for her footwear or the crime scene. It had certainly washed away any tracks, and it'd sent a stream of ashes down the hill from the cabin. The black soot slivered through the crushed limestone, creating an eerie effect.

Reed said something to the uniformed officer and then looked at her. He motioned for Livvy to follow. Despite the mud weights now on her soles, she did. Not easily though. Reed began to plow through the woods like a man on a mission.

"They found something," he relayed to her without even looking back to make sure she was there.

That got Livvy moving faster, and she followed him

through the maze of wet branches, underbrush and wildflowers. "What?"

But Reed didn't answer. He made his way to some yellow crime-scene tape that had been tied to a scrawny mesquite oak. "They didn't collect it," he explained. "They figured you'd want to do that."

Livvy walked around the tree and examined what had caused Reed to react the way he had. It didn't take her long to see the swatch of fabric clinging to a low-hanging branch. It was fairly large, at least two inches long and an inch wide. She immediately set down her equipment bag and took out the supplies she needed to photograph and tag it. Thank goodness she had a backup camera because her primary one was destroyed in the fire.

"It looks as if it came from the cuff of a shirt," Reed pointed out.

Possibly. It was thick, maybe double-layered, and there was enough cloth for her to see that it was multi-colored with thin stripes of dark gold and burgundy on a navy blue background. It wouldn't have been her first choice of clothing to wear to commit a crime because the pattern really stood out.

Livvy snapped pictures of the swatch from different angles. "Did you see the perp's clothing when he was by my SUV and then running into the woods?"

"Just the baseball cap. But it's possible he had on a jacket, and that's why I didn't see the shirt."

Yes, or maybe this didn't belong to the suspect. Still, Livvy continued to hope because something like this could literally solve the case.

"You think it has DNA on it?" Reed asked.

"It might. If not on the fabric itself, then maybe the

tree branch snagged some skin." It looked as if the fabric had been ripped off while someone was running past the branch.

Reed got closer, practically arm to arm with her, and took his own photograph using his cell phone. "I'm sending this to Kirby at the office." He pressed some buttons on his phone to do that. "I'll have him ask around and see if anyone recognizes the fabric."

Good idea. She wished she'd thought of it first, and then Livvy scolded herself for even going there. Reed and she were on the same side, and maybe if she repeated it enough, she would soon believe it. She certainly wasn't having trouble remembering everything else about him.

Livvy finished the photographing, bagged the fabric and then snipped the tip of the branch so she could bag it as well. While she did that, Reed walked deeper into the woods.

"See anything else?" she asked.

"No." He stopped, propped his hands on his hips and looked around. "But if I were going to commit a crime and then make a fast escape, this is the route I'd go. If he'd gone east, that would have put him on the road. There's a creek to the west, and this time of year it's swollen because of the spring rains. With the fire and us behind him, this was the only way out."

Picking up the equipment bag, she went closer. "So, you're thinking the person was local?"

He nodded. And remained in deep thought for several long moments. "Jonah doesn't exactly encourage people to go traipsing onto his land, so there aren't paths through here." Reed pointed to the even thicker brush and trees ahead. "And once the arsonist made it to that point, I wouldn't have been able to see him. If that fabric belongs to him and if he ran in a fairly straight line, he would have ended up there."

Reed pointed to a trio of oaks standing so close together they were practically touching. Around them were thick clumps of cedars.

"The deputies searched that area?" Livvy asked.

Reed glanced around at the tracks on the muddy ground. "Yeah. But I'd like to have another look."

So would she, so Livvy followed him. She checked for breakage on the branches and shrubs, but when she didn't see any, she went farther to her right because the perp could have wavered from a straight-line run, especially once he was aware that Reed was in pursuit.

Since any point could be the escape route, she took some pictures, the flash of the camera slicing through the morning light. She was aware of the sound of Reed's footsteps, but Livvy continued to photograph the scene while moving right.

"Stop!" Reed shouted. But he didn't just shout.

He grabbed on to her shoulder and jerked her back so that she landed hard against his chest. Suddenly she was touching him everywhere and was in his arms.

"What are you doing?" she managed to ask. She looked up at him, but Reed's attention wasn't on her. It was on the ground.

"Trap." He pointed to a clump of soggy decaying leaves.

Livvy didn't understand at first, but she followed Reed's pointing finger and spotted the bit of black metal poking out from the clump.

Reed reached down, picked up a rock and tossed it at the device. It snapped shut, the claw-like sides closing in as they were meant to capture whatever—or who-ever—was unfortunate enough to step on it. If she'd walked just another few inches, that trap would have clamped on to her foot.

"The perp probably wouldn't have had time to set that," Livvy managed to say. Not easily. Her heart was pounding and her breath had gone so thin that she could barely speak.

"Not unless he put it here before he started the fires."

Yes, and if he'd done that, then this crime had been premeditated. Worse, if there was one trap, there might be others.

"I need an evidence bag," Reed told her, moving toward the trap. "The trap might have fingerprints on it."

Livvy handed him a large collection bag and watched as he carefully retrieved the trap. "I'll have the deputies go through the area with a metal detector. After we're sure it's safe, we'll come back and keep looking."

She wasn't about to argue with that. First the fires. Then, Reed's encounter with the rental car. Now, this. It didn't take any CSI training to know that someone didn't want them to investigate this case.

Reed's cell phone rang, and he handed her the bagged trap so that he could take the call. Livvy labeled the item and eased it into her evidence bag so that she wouldn't smear any prints or DNA that might be on it.

"Billy said what?" Reed asked. And judging from his suddenly sharp tone, he wasn't pleased about something.

Since she couldn't actually hear what the caller was

saying, she watched Reed's expression and it went from bad to worse.

"What's wrong?" she asked the moment he ended the call.

Reed turned and started back toward his truck. "Kirby faxed the picture of the fabric to all the town agencies, and Billy Whitley said he'd seen that pattern before, and that it'd come from a shirt."

Billy Whitley. The county clerk she'd met in front of the sheriff's office the day before. The one who might also have ties to Marcie and her murder. "And did Billy happen to know who owns that shirt?"

"Yeah, he did." That was all Reed said until they made it back into the clearing. "Come on. We need to question a suspect."

Chapter Seven

Reed pulled to a stop at the end of the tree-lined private road that led to Jonah Becker's sprawling ranch house. He couldn't drive any farther because someone had closed and locked the wrought-iron cattle gates. Since he'd called about fifteen minutes earlier to let Jonah know he was on the way to have a *chat*, Reed figured the surly rancher had shut the gates on purpose.

It wouldn't keep Reed out.

Livvy and he could simply use the narrow footpath to the side of the gates. But it would mean a quarter-mile walk to question Jonah about how the devil a piece of his shirt had gotten torn on a tree branch mere yards from a double crime scene.

Though he figured it was futile, Reed called the ranch again and this time got the housekeeper. When he asked her to open the gate, she mumbled something about her boss saying it was to stay shut for the day. She further mumbled there was trouble with some of the calves getting out.

Right.

Jonah just wanted to make this as hard as possible.

Even though Reed hadn't specifically mentioned the shirt fabric they'd found, Jonah no doubt suspected something was up, and that *something* wasn't going to work in his favor. Of course, the real question was—had Jonah really committed a felony by burning Livvy's SUV and destroying evidence at a crime scene? And if the answer to that was yes, then Reed also had to consider him a candidate for Marcie's murder.

Livvy and he got out of the truck and started the trek along the deeply curved road. Thankfully, the road was paved so once they made it through the turnstile pedestrian gate, they didn't have to continue to use the muddy ground or pastures that fanned out for miles on each side of the ranch.

"It's a big place," Livvy commented, while shifting her equipment bag that had to weigh at least twenty-five pounds, especially now that it had the trap inside.

Reed figured it would result in a glare, but he reached out and took the bag from her. He waited for the argument about her being able to do it herself, but she simply mumbled "Thanks."

"Thanks?" he repeated.

Her mouth quivered a little. A smile threatened. "This doesn't mean anything. Well, other than you're stronger than I am."

But the smile that finally bent her mouth told him it might be more than that. The slight change of heart was reasonable. They were spending nearly every waking moment together, and they were both focused on the case. That created camaraderie. A friendship, almost. It definitely created a bond because they were on the same side.

Reed frowned. And wondered why he felt the need to justify his attraction to a good-looking woman. True, he hadn't planned on an attraction that might result in a relationship, but he was coming to terms with the notion that not having something in his plans didn't mean it wasn't going to happen anyway.

"Hold up a minute," Livvy said. She picked up a stick and used it to scrape some of the mud from those city heels on her boots.

"Those boots aren't very practical out here," Reed commented.

"No. My good pair was lost with some luggage when I was visiting my dad. I ordered another pair last night off the Internet, and I'm hoping they'll get here today."

So, this wasn't normal for her. What was, exactly? And what did she wear when she wasn't in her usual Ranger "uniform" of jeans and a white shirt? While Reed was thinking about that, he realized she'd stopped scraping mud and was staring at him.

"We, uh, both started off with some misconceptions about each other," she admitted.

"You're still from New York," he teased. But Reed immediately regretted his attempt at humor. He saw the darkness creep into her eyes and realized he'd hit a nerve. "Sorry."

"No. It's okay." She looked down and started to scrape at the mud again.

Since she wobbled and seemed on the verge of losing her balance, Reed caught on to her arm. He immediately felt her muscles tense. And her eyes met his again. Not a stare this time. Just a brief glance. But a lot of things passed between them with that glance.

Both of them cursed.

It'd been stupid to touch her, and Reed upped the ante on that stupidity by moving in closer still, lowering his head and putting his mouth on hers. Reed expected profanity. Maybe even a slap. He certainly deserved it, and a slap might just knock some sense into him.

But Livvy didn't curse or slap him.

She made a sound of pleasure, deep within her chest. It was brief and soft, barely there, but she might as well have shouted that the kiss was good for her, too. It was certainly *good* for Reed. Her mouth was like silk and, in that kiss, he took in her breath and taste.

That taste went straight through him.

And for just a moment he had a too-vivid image of what it would be like to kiss her harder and deeper. To push her against the nearby oak and do things he'd wanted to do since the first time he'd laid eyes on her.

Now, Livvy cursed and jerked away from him. "I know what you're thinking," she grumbled.

Hell. He hoped not. "What?"

"You're thinking that was unprofessional."

"Uh, no. Actually, I was thinking you taste even better than I thought you would, and my expectations were pretty damn high."

The smile threatened again, but it was quickly followed by a full-fledged scowl that she seemed to be aiming at herself. Livvy grabbed the equipment bag from him and started marching toward the ranch house.

"I have to do a good job here," she said when Reed fell in step alongside her. "I have to prove I can handle a complex crime scene on my own."

Reed understood the pressure, though he had never

experienced it firsthand. "It's been the opposite for me," he admitted. "My father was the sheriff so folks around here just accepted that I was the best man for the job."

"Lucky you." But she didn't say it as a snippy insult. More like envy.

"Well, maybe that luck will rub off on you." Which sounded sexual. His body was still begging for him to kiss her again. That would be a bad idea, especially since they were now close to the ranch house.

Livvy must have realized that as well because she looked ahead at the massive estate that peeked through the trees. "Jonah will probably try to convince us that the fabric's been there for a long time."

"Probably. But it hadn't been there long because it showed no signs of wear or of being exposed to the elements."

Jonah would try to refute that as well, but the man was still going to have a hard time explaining how he tore his shirt in that part of the woods, just yards from a murder scene.

As they got closer, Reed saw Jonah. He was waiting for them on the front porch.

And he wasn't alone.

Jonah's daughter, Jessie, had just served her father and his guest some iced tea. She tipped her head toward them in greeting.

"Don't work yourself up into a state," Jessie told her father, and she gently touched his arm. Her gaze came back to Reed, and she seemed to issue him a be-nice warning before she disappeared into the house.

Seated in a white wicker chair next to Jonah was a sandy-haired man Reed knew all too well: Jerry Collier.

"He's the head of the Comanche Creek Land Office," Livvy pointed out.

Reed nodded. "Jerry was also Marcie's former boss. And on various occasions, he acts as Jonah's attorney."

"Jonah lawyered up," she grumbled.

Apparently. And that was probably wise on Jonah's part. The man's temper often got in the way of his reason, and he must have guessed something incriminating had turned up.

"Reed," Jerry snapped, getting to his feet. Everything about him was nervous and defensive. That doubled when he turned his narrowed dust-gray eyes on Livvy. "Sergeant Hutton. I'm guessing you're responsible for this visit because Reed knows Jonah didn't have anything to do with what went on in his cabin."

"Is that true?" Livvy asked the rancher.

Jonah stayed seated and didn't seem nearly as ruffled as Jerry. "I understand you found a piece of cloth."

Reed groaned and didn't even bother to ask who'd told the man, but he'd ask Kirby about it later. His deputy apparently hadn't kept quiet as Reed had ordered.

Livvy set the equipment bag on the porch steps and took out the bagged swatch of fabric. She held it up for the men to see. "Does this belong to you?"

"Don't answer that," Jerry insisted. He wagged his finger at Reed. "First you accuse Woody of wrongdoing, and now Jonah? Am I next?"

"That's entirely possible," Reed calmly answered. "The investigation's not over. Who knows what I'll be able to dig up about you."

"And everybody else in town?" Jerry tossed back.

"No. Just the folks with motive to kill Marcie. Like you, for instance. I can't imagine you were happy when she showed up, ready to testify against you. And you couldn't have been pleased about it, either," Reed added, tipping his head toward Jonah.

Jerry aimed his comments at Livvy. "Marcie could testify all she wanted, but that doesn't mean Jonah and I did anything wrong."

"You're talking to the wrong person," Jonah told his lawyer. A faint smile bent the corner of Jonah's mouth. "Reed's in charge of this investigation, aren't you? The Rangers don't have a lot of faith in Sergeant Hutton."

Reed didn't have to look at Livvy to know that brought on a glare.

"Oh, they trust her," Reed corrected before Livvy could get into a battle of words with Jonah and Jerry. "The only reason I'm in charge is because the Rangers believe I know folks around here well enough that I can help Livvy get to the truth. And one way or another, we will get to the truth," Reed warned.

Jerry motioned toward the road. "You're looking for truth in the wrong place. Neither one of us had anything to do with Marcie's death."

Reed stepped closer, making sure he got way too close to Jerry. He knew Jerry wouldn't like that. For lack of a better word, the man was anal. Everything in its place. Everything *normal*. It wouldn't be normal for Reed to get in his face.

"Jerry, if I thought for one minute you were innocent in all of this, I wouldn't be talking to you. I believe you're just one step above being a snake-oil salesman. *One step*," Reed emphasized, showing him a very narrow space between his thumb and index finger. "And I think you'd kill Marcie in a New York minute and then come here and pretend that you need to defend your old friend Jonah."

That caused the veins to bulge on Jerry's forehead, and he opened his mouth, no doubt to return verbal fire.

"Jerry, why don't you head back to your office?" Jonah ordered. "Just use the code I gave you to open the gate."

"I'd rather stay here," Jerry insisted, glaring at Reed.

Jonah angled his eyes in Jerry's direction. "And I'd rather you didn't. Go ahead. Head on out."

But Jerry didn't. Not right away. It took Jerry turning to Jonah, probably to plead his case as to why he should stay, but Jonah's eyes held no promise of compromise.

"Leave now," Jonah growled.

That sent Jerry cursing and storming off the porch and toward his silver-gray Mercedes. He gave Reed and Livvy one last glare before he got in, slammed the door and sped off.

Jonah calmly picked up his glass of iced tea and had a sip. He looked at Reed over the top of his glass that was beaded with moisture. "That fabric you found—it came from a shirt I used to own."

"Used to own?" Livvy questioned.

Jonah lazily set the glass aside as if he had all the time in the world. "I did some spring cleaning about two weeks ago and sent a bunch of old clothes to the charity rummage sale the church put on. That shirt was just one of the things I donated."

Well, there *had* been a rummage sale two weeks ago, but Reed had never known Jonah to be a charitable man.

"You donated it," Livvy repeated. "That's convenient."

"It's the truth." Jonah didn't smile, but there was a smug look on his face. He took a folded piece of paper from his pocket and handed it to Reed. "That's a copy of the things I donated."

Reed glanced over the dozen or so items, all clothing, and there were indeed three shirts listed on the tax receipt form.

Livvy leaned over and looked at it as well. "I don't suppose the church group would know who bought the shirt."

"No need," Jonah said before Reed could answer. "I already know because I saw him wearing it in town just a couple of days ago. I guess some people don't have any trouble with hand-me-downs."

Reed waited. And waited. But it was obvious Jonah was going to make him ask. "Who bought the shirt?"

"Shane's father, Ben Tolbert."

If Jonah had said any other name, Reed would have questioned it, but Ben probably did buy his clothing at rummage sales. Better yet, Ben had a powerful motive for burning down that cabin and Livvy's SUV.

Shane.

Ben wasn't a model citizen, but no one in Comanche Creek could doubt that he loved his son. Add to that, Ben did have a record and had been arrested several times. Nothing as serious as this, though.

"I already called Ben," Jonah continued, "and he didn't answer his phone. When you get a chance to talk to him, tell him I'm none too happy with him burning down my place and that I'm filing charges. I want his butt in a jail cell next to his murdering son."

Reed figured it was a good thing that Jonah's own

son, Trace, wasn't around to hear his dad call Shane a killer. Trace and Shane had been friends since childhood, and Reed knew for a fact that Trace believed Shane to be innocent and had even tried to pay for a big-time lawyer to be brought in if the case went to trial.

"If I find out you're lying about Ben having the shirt, then you'll be the one in a jail cell next to Shane," Reed warned.

"And I'll be the one right there to make sure you're fired," Jonah warned back. "I won't be railroaded into taking the blame for something your own deputy and his loony father have done."

Since Reed knew there was no benefit to continuing this discussion, he turned and motioned for Livvy to follow him. "I need to talk to Ben before I go any further with this," Reed told her when they were a few yards away from the porch. He could practically feel Jonah staring holes in his back.

"If Ben doesn't corroborate Jonah's story about the shirt, will you be able to get a search warrant?" Livvy asked.

"Yeah. But it wouldn't do any good. If Jonah set those fires, then trust me, that shirt is long gone."

"True. He doesn't seem like the kind of man to keep incriminating evidence lying around." Livvy shrugged. "Which makes me wonder why he would have worn such a recognizable shirt to commit a crime."

Reed could think of a reason—to throw suspicion off himself by drawing attention to himself. A sort of reverse psychology. Still, that didn't mean Jonah hadn't hired someone to wear that shirt and destroy the evidence.

"I'll talk to Shane," Reed assured her. "He might know something about all of this."

"And he'd be willing to incriminate his father?"

"He has in the past. Three years ago when Ben got drunk and trashed some cars in the parking lot of the Longhorn Bar, Shane arrested him."

"Yes, but this is different. This is a felony. His father could go to jail for years."

Reed couldn't argue with that. But if Shane couldn't or wouldn't verify the shirt issue, then there were other ways to get at the truth, even if it meant questioning everyone in town.

"Look," Livvy said. She pointed to a storage barn in the pasture to their right.

Reed immediately saw what had captured her attention. There were several traps hanging on hooks. Traps that looked identical to the one someone had set near the cabin.

"You think they'll have serial numbers or something on them to link them to the other one?" she asked.

"Possibly. But even if they do and if they match the one we found, Jonah could say he set the trap because he owned the property and was having trouble with coyotes or something."

She shook her head. "But I have the feeling the trap was set for us. For me," Livvy softly added. "Someone in Comanche Creek doesn't want us to learn the truth about what happened to Marcie."

Reed had a bad feeling that she was right.

He thought about her alone at night in the inn and considered repeating his offer for her to stay at his place. She'd refuse, of course. Probably because she knew that would lead to a different kind of trouble. But even at the risk of Livvy landing in his bed, he wanted to do more to make sure she stayed safe while working on this case.

Reed mentally stopped.

Cursed.

"What's wrong?" Livvy asked, firing glances all around as if she expected them to be ambushed.

Reed wasn't sure this would sound any better aloud than it did in his head. "I'm thinking about staying at the inn. Just until this case is wrapped up."

She stopped, turned and stared at him. "And the profanity wasn't because of the element of danger. You know that being under the same roof with me isn't a good idea."

He tried to shrug. "Depends on what you consider a good idea."

Her stare turned flat. "Having a one-night stand with you wouldn't be a good idea. Or even a two-night stand, for that matter. Besides, you wouldn't even make the offer to stay at the inn if I were a man."

"True," he readily admitted. "But if you were a man, I wouldn't be torn between wanting you and protecting you."

She huffed and started to walk again. She was trying to dismiss all of this. But Reed figured the time for dismissing was long gone.

"My advice?" she said, her voice all breathy and hot. "We forget that kiss ever happened."

"Right." And he hoped his dry tone conveyed his skepticism. He'd have an easier time forgetting that he was neck-deep in a murder investigation. "We'll head back to the jail and talk to Shane about his father."

And once they'd done that, he'd think about his possible upcoming stay at the inn.

The cattle gates were wide open when they approached them. Jerry had no doubt left in a huff, especially since Jonah had essentially told him to get lost. That was something else Reed needed to give some thought. If Jonah hadn't wanted Jerry there in the first place, then what had the man been doing at Jonah's ranch? Reed trusted Jerry even less than he did Jonah, and he hoped Jerry hadn't made the visit because he had something to plot with Jonah.

Or something to hide.

They passed through the gate just as his phone rang. From the caller ID, he could see that it was Kirby.

"Don't tell me something else has gone wrong," Reed answered.

"No. Well, not that I know of anyway. I still haven't been able to reach Ben Tolbert like you asked. But I did just get a call from the crime lab about the gun Shane was holding when he was found standing over Marcie's body."

Reed took a deep breath and put the call on speaker so Livvy could hear this as well.

"That gun was the murder weapon," Kirby confirmed.

Hell. Reed glanced at Livvy. No I-told-you-so look on her face. Instead, her forehead was creased as if she were deep in thought.

"They also IDed the gun owner. A dealer in San Antonio who said he sold the piece over a week ago to a man named Adam Smith."

Reed shook his head. "Let me guess—Adam Smith doesn't exist."

"You're right. The documents he provided for proof of identity are all fake."

So, either Shane had faked them, or this was looking more and more like a complex, premeditated murder of a person who could have been a potential witness against both Jonah and Jerry for their involvement in that shady land deal.

Yeah. Reed really needed to do some more digging on both men.

"Kirby, could you please have the lab courier the murder weapon back to Reed's office?" Livvy asked. "I want to take a look at that gun."

"It's already on the way. Your boss figured you'd want to examine it so he sent it with the courier about an hour ago. Should be here any minute."

"Thank you."

Reed hung up and opened the door so that he could toss in Livvy's equipment bag. He heard the sound.

The too-familiar rattle.

And he reacted just as much from fear as he did instinct. He pushed Livvy to the side.

It wasn't a second too soon.

Because the diamondback rattler that was coiled on the seat sprang right at them.

Chapter Eight

Everything was a blur. One minute Livvy was getting ready to step inside the truck, and the next, she was on the ground.

She heard the rattling sound, and it turned her blood to ice. Livvy rolled to her side and scrambled to get away.

The rattler shot out of the truck again, aiming for a second attempt to strike them, and she shouted for Reed to move. He did. And in the same motion, he drew his gun.

And fired.

The shot blasted through the countryside, and he followed it up with a second one. That didn't stop the snake. Livvy watched in horror as the rattler made a third strike. Its fangs stabbed right into Reed's leather shoulder holster. He threw it off, fired a fourth shot, and this time the bullet hit its intended target.

Still, the snake didn't stop moving. It continued to coil and rattle before it slithered away.

"Did it bite you?" Livvy managed to ask. Her heart felt as if it were literally in her throat.

Reed shook his head and looked at her. "Are you okay?"

She took a moment to assess her situation. "I'm fine, but what about you?" Livvy got to her feet and checked out his arm and shoulder.

"I wasn't hurt." He checked her out as well, and when his gaze landed on her now-muddy jeans and shirt, he cursed. "This wasn't an accident. That snake didn't open my truck door and crawl in."

No. And that meant someone had put it there. "Who would do this?"

"The same person who's been trying to make our lives hell for the past two days." He paused to curse again. "The snake probably wouldn't have killed us even with multiple bites, and the town doc keeps a supply of antivenom. But it would have made us very sick and put us out of commission for God knows how long."

"And it scared us. Scared *me,*" she corrected. Livvy flicked the loose bits of mud off her clothes. "But it won't scare me enough to stop this investigation."

"No, it won't," Reed readily agreed. He checked his watch, eyed the truck and then eyed her. "You think you can get inside?"

She could. Livvy had no doubts about that, but she couldn't quite control her body's response to nearly being the victim of a snake attack.

"You believe Ben Tolbert is capable of this?" Livvy took a deep breath and got inside.

Reed did the same, and he started the engine. "He's capable all right. Rattlesnakes aren't exactly hard to find around here, and some people trap and sell them.

There's a trapper about twenty miles from here who runs a rattlesnake roundup. I'll call him and see if anyone's recently purchased a diamondback from him."

It would be a necessary call, just to cover all bases, but Livvy doubted the culprit would go that route where he could be easily identified. "What about Jerry Collier? He left the ranch house in plenty of time to plant the snake."

Reed nodded. "And he was riled enough to do it."

Yes, he was. "But that would indicate premeditation."

"Maybe. Or maybe he spotted the snake as he was driving out and did it on the spur of the moment."

She tried to imagine the suit-wearing, nervous head of the Comanche Creek Land Office doing something like picking up a live rattler on a muddy road, but it didn't seem logical. Well, not logical in her downtown office in Austin, but out here, anything seemed plausible.

"Don't worry—I'll question Jerry," Reed continued, his voice as tight as the grip he now had on the steering wheel. "Ben, too. And I'll have the outside of the truck dusted for prints. We might get lucky."

"I'm sorry," he added a moment later.

Since his tone had just as much anger as apology, she looked at him. Yes, he was riled. Maybe it was simply because of the leftover adrenaline from the attack, but Livvy got the impression that he was angry because of her, because she'd been placed in danger.

And because there was now *something* between them. Something more than the job.

She was about to remind him that the kiss and attraction really couldn't play into this, but he grabbed his phone from his pocket, scrolled down through the recent calls he'd made and pressed the call button.

"I want to speak to Jerry," Reed demanded of who-ever answered. There was at least a five-second pause. "Then take a message. He needs to call me immediately, or else I'll arrest his sorry ass."

Reed ended that call and made another. This time, he put it on speaker, and she heard the call go straight to Ben Tolbert's voice mail. Reed issued another threat-ening order very similar to the one he'd left for Jerry. But he didn't stop there. Reed continued to call around: to the mayor, then someone on the city board, and he asked both men to help him locate Jerry Collier and Ben Tolbert. He was still making calls when he pulled to a stop in the parking lot of his office.

Livvy knew it wasn't a good time to be close to Reed, not with so much emotion still zinging around and between them, so she grabbed her equipment bag, got out of the truck and, with Reed right behind her, she hurried inside.

Eileen, the receptionist, gave her a warm smile and a hello. Livvy tried to return the greeting but wasn't pleased to hear the tremble in her voice. Her hands were shaking, too, and since she didn't want to risk a meltdown in front of anyone, she mumbled something that she hoped would sound composed and raced into Reed's office.

Livvy hurried to the desk that he'd set up for her to work, and she took out the trap and fabric swatch so she could start the paperwork to send them to the lab in Austin.

It also gave her hands and her mind something to do.

She wasn't a coward and knew full well that danger was part of the job, but she wasn't immune to the effects of coming so close to Reed and her being hurt.

She heard the door shut and glanced over her shoulder at Reed. He stood there as if trying to collect himself, a response she totally understood.

"Here are the trap and the fabric," she said. Her voice was still shaky, and Livvy cleared her throat hoping it would help. "When the courier gets here with the murder weapon, I'll have him go ahead and take the items to the crime lab for testing."

Livvy picked up a note. A message left for her by Kirby. She read it out loud: "'The lab checked on the number I gave them for the missing phone. It was one of those prepaid cells, and the person who bought it must have paid cash because there's no record of purchase. That means we can't trace the buyer, and we won't be able to find out about any calls he might have made.'"

Reed didn't respond to that latest dose of disappointing news. Instead, he reached behind him, locked the door and pushed himself away. But he did more than just walk toward her. When he reached her, he latched on to her arm and hauled her against him. Reed pulled her into a tight embrace.

"I'll try very hard not to let something like that happen again," he said.

Confused, Livvy looked up at him. "You mean the snake or the kiss?"

He smiled, but it was short-lived and there was no humor in it. "The snake."

Yes, but both were dangerous in their own way, and Reed and she knew that. Still, Livvy didn't move away, even when he slid his arm around her waist and pulled her closer. Not even when her breasts pressed against his chest. Not even when she felt his warm breath push through the wisps of her hair.

Livvy could have sworn the air changed between them. The nerves and adrenaline were still there, but she felt another emotion creep into the already volatile mix.

Attraction.

Yes, it was there, too, and all the talk and head-shaking in the world wouldn't make it go away. She opened her mouth to say, well, she had no idea what to say. But despite the hot attraction, she knew she had to say or do something to stop the escalation of all these crazy emotions.

But she didn't stop it.

Instead, she did the opposite. She came up on her tiptoes...

And she kissed him.

Not a peck, either, like the other one at the ranch, though it started that way. Reed took things from there. He made sure this one was hard, French.

And memorable.

Livvy didn't do anything to stop this either, despite the intense argument going on between her head and the rest of her body. No. She made things better—and worse—by slinging her arm around his neck and moving even closer.

That taste.

It was amazing. And the man moved over her mouth as if he owned her. She did her own share of kiss-deepening as well, and they didn't break the intimate contact until they both realized they needed to catch their breaths.

Reed looked stunned and confused when he drew

back. Livvy knew how he felt. They were both in a lot of trouble, and she didn't think they'd be getting out of this trouble any time soon.

"The evidence," she said as a reminder to both herself and Reed.

"Yeah." Still, he didn't pull away. He pressed his forehead against hers and groaned. "I would promise not to do that again, but you and I both know it's a promise I can't keep."

"We can't just land in bed, either." Though that suddenly seemed like a great idea. Sheez. Her body really wasn't being very professional.

Now, he smiled and looked down at her. "The bed is optional. Sex with you? Not so optional." He pressed harder against her. So hard that she could feel the proof of their attraction. "I want you bad, Livvy, and all the logic and the danger in the world won't wish that away."

That seemed to be a challenge, as if he expected her to dispute what he was saying. She couldn't.

The sound of his ringing cell phone shot through the room, and that sent them flying apart. Good. They weren't totally stupid.

Just yet, anyway.

"Kirby?" he answered after glancing at the caller ID screen.

Livvy welcomed the reprieve. Well, part of her did anyway. But she knew it was just that: a reprieve. Somehow, she would have to force herself away from Reed. Maybe she could move her side of the investigation to the inn, just so they wouldn't be elbow to elbow. That might minimize the temptation of the mouth-to-mouth contact.

But then she looked at him.

All six feet plus of him. With that rumpled dark hair and bedroom eyes, he wasn't the sort of man that a woman could *minimize*.

"As soon as he steps foot in his office, let me know. Thanks, Kirby." He closed his phone and shoved it into his pocket. He tipped his head to the fabric and trap. "I'll have Eileen arrange to have that taken to the crime lab, but it might not happen before we get to question Jerry. He's on his way back to his office."

"Good. We can ask him about the rattlesnake." Livvy put the evidence into the locker so it would be safe until the courier arrived.

"We can ask him more than that. Kirby just learned the results from the footprint castings that you took. And they're a perfect match to Jerry Collier."

Livvy sank down into the chair just a few inches from her worktable. "Is there any valid reason why his footprints would be there?"

"None that I know of. Plus, he has one of the strongest motives for wanting Marcie dead. If she had managed to stay alive long enough to testify against him, Jerry would have ended up in jail. Without her testimony, the state doesn't have a strong enough case."

That was a huge motive indeed, and Livvy was about to use her laptop to request a full background check on Jerry, but there was a knock at the door. Reed crossed the room, unlocked the door, and when he opened it, Kirby was standing there. The young deputy looked puzzled and maybe even suspicious as to why the door had been locked.

Great.

If Kirby sensed the attraction between Reed and her, God knew how little time it would take to get around town. She was betting everyone would know by lunchtime.

Livvy took the bagged and tagged gun from Kirby and initialed the chain of custody form. He also handed her the report file from the lab. While Kirby and Reed discussed whether or not they should issue an APB for Ben Tolbert, Livvy put on her gloves and got to work examining the gun.

It was a Ruger .22 Rimfire pistol. Common and inexpensive. A person could buy it for under three hundred dollars at any gun store in the state. Just about anyone who wanted a gun badly enough could afford it.

Including all of their suspects.

The Ruger had already been processed, and even though it was indeed the murder weapon, according to the report, it contained no DNA. Just fingerprints that had been dusted and photographed. The photographs had then been fed into AFIS, the Automated Fingerprint Identification System. The result?

They were Shane's prints.

The fact there was no DNA was odd, especially since the lab had run a touch test, which should have been able to detect even a minute amount of biological material.

Yet, nothing.

Since Shane had supposedly shot Marcie at close range, there should have been some blood spatter or maybe even sweat from Shane's hand. First-time killers normally weren't so calm and cool that they didn't leave a piece of themselves behind at the crime scene.

She set the gun aside, and went through the report file. There were several photos of the fingerprints on the weapon, and the tech who'd taken them had been thorough. Livvy could see the placement of every print, including the one on the trigger, which had a much lighter point of pressure than the others.

Also odd.

It should have been about the same, or maybe even heavier. Killers didn't usually have such a light touch when it came to pulling a trigger.

She picked up the gun again and took a magnifying glass from her case so she could look at the actual pattern. Even though some of the fingerprint powder and the prints themselves had been smeared during transport and processing, she could still see where the shooter had gripped the gun. That created a vivid image in her mind.

Shane pointing the gun at Marcie.

Then firing.

Livvy replayed the scene again. And again. Each time, she made tiny mental changes to see if she could recreate the end result: Marcie's murder with Shane pulling the trigger.

"Something about this doesn't look right," she mumbled. She glanced over her shoulder to see if Reed had heard her, but his attention wasn't on her. It was on the phone call that he'd just answered.

"Good, because we want to talk to you, too," Reed snarled. But his expression morphed into concern. "We'll be right there."

"What happened?" Livvy asked when he slapped the phone shut.

"That was Jerry Collier, and he's back in his office. He says someone is out to kill you, and he knows who that person is."

Chapter Nine

"If you'd rather stay at the office and finish examining the gun, I can do this alone," Reed offered, though he knew what Livvy's answer would be.

"No, thanks." Her response was crisp and fast, like the speed at which she exited the building. "I'd like to learn the identity of the person who wants me dead."

So would Reed, but he wasn't certain they would be getting that information from Jerry. Still, he wasn't about to pass up the opportunity to question the man about the dangerous attempts that had been orchestrated to prevent Livvy and him from doing their jobs.

They went into the parking lot, and he spotted one of the loaner deputies who was examining his truck for prints and other evidence. Reed didn't want to interrupt that or destroy any potential evidence by using the vehicle. The other deputies were apparently still at the crime scene or else on patrol because his official vehicle was nowhere in sight. That left the one cruiser, which Reed hated to tie up in case Kirby had to respond to an emergency.

The Comanche Creek Land Office was just up the

street about a quarter of a mile away, but it wouldn't be a comfortable stroll. It was already turning into a scorcher day with the heat and humidity. Plus, there was the potential danger, which mostly seemed to be aimed at Livvy. Maybe it wasn't wise to have her out in the open.

"It'd be safer if I have someone drive us," Reed suggested.

She looked at him as if he'd sprouted a third eye. "I won't let this scare me. We're both peace officers, and if we can't walk down the street in broad daylight without being afraid, then that sends a message to the perp that I don't want to send."

And with that, she started walking again. "Besides, I need a few minutes to clear my head," Livvy added. "I don't want to go storming into Jerry's office like this."

Reed was on the same page with her. First, the footprints that were a match to Jerry, and then his bombshell comment about knowing who wanted to kill Livvy. Up to this point, Reed had hoped and believed that the incidents were meant to scare her off. Not kill her. But by God, if that was someone's intention, then there'd be hell to pay.

He didn't curse himself or groan at that thought. Somewhere along the way, he'd crossed the line with Livvy, and cursing and groaning weren't going to make him backtrack even if that was the sensible thing to do.

"You said there was no gunshot residue anywhere on Shane?" she asked, pulling him out of a fit of temper that was building because of Jerry.

"None. Why?"

She lifted her shoulder. "I've just been trying to get the picture straight in my mind."

Yeah. He'd done that as well, and this was one picture that hadn't fit right from the start. Well, unless Shane truly was a cold-blooded killer who'd set all of this up.

"You make a fine-looking couple," someone called out.

Reed glanced across the street and spotted Billy Whitley, the county clerk, and his wife, Charla, who were just going into the diner, probably for an early lunch.

"Careful," Billy teased. "People will say you're in love."

Reed stopped to set him straight, but Charla got in on the conversation.

Charla nudged her elbow into Billy's ribs. "I know you got better sense than that, Reed," Charla countered. "That woman's trying to tear this town apart."

"Actually, I'm just trying to do my job," Livvy fired back.

That earned Livvy a *hmmmp* from Charla, and the woman threw open the door of the diner and stormed inside. Billy gave an apologetic wave and followed her.

Reed didn't know which was worse—Billy's innuendo or Charla's obvious dislike of Livvy. "Sorry," he mumbled to Livvy once they started walking again.

"No need to apologize. Will this cause trouble for you?" she asked but didn't wait for his answer. "Would it be better if we did separate investigations?"

Reed didn't even have to think about this. "It wouldn't help. You're a woman and I'm a man. We're both single. If people don't see us together, they'll just say we're staying apart so we don't raise suspicions about a secret relationship."

And that was really all he wanted to say about that, especially since the gossip was really going to heat up because Reed planned to spend a lot more time with her at work and at the inn.

Reed would break that news to Livvy later.

"We were discussing the gun," he prompted.

"Yes." She wiped the perspiration from her forehead and repeated it. "I think there's a problem with the pressure points. The print isn't that strong on the trigger."

Despite the heat, Reed slowed a bit so he could give that some thought. Now, he got that picture in his mind. "The person who hit Shane over the head could have used gloves when he shot Marcie. Then, he could have pressed Shane's prints onto the weapon."

Hell. Why hadn't he thought of that sooner? Probably because this case had come at him nonstop. It was almost as if someone wanted to make sure that his focus was disrupted. Maybe that was the real reason for all the diversions, like that snake.

"I need to do some further testing," Livvy added. Her forehead creased. "It could mean that Shane just has a light touch when it comes to his trigger finger. I'd like to compare this weapon to his service pistol, just to see how the grip pattern lines up."

That would give her information if Shane hadn't recently cleaned his gun. For the first time in Reed's law-enforcement career, he was hoping his deputy had been lax about that particular standard procedure. "You can do that as soon as we finish with Jerry because I have his gun locked up in the safe in my office."

Ahead of them on the steps to the county offices were three men and a woman, all Native Americans, and all carrying signs of protest.

"Sheriff Hardin," the woman called out, and her tone wasn't friendly, either. Not that Reed expected it to be, since she was carrying a big poster that demanded justice for her people.

"Ellie," Reed greeted her. He caught onto Livvy's arm and tried to maneuver her around the protesters, but the trim Comanche woman, Ellie Penateka, stepped in front of them.

Reed had known Ellie all his life, and though she was passionate about her beliefs, she could also toe the line of the law.

"When will you do your job and arrest Jonah Becker and his cronies?" Ellie demanded.

"When I have some evidence that warrants an arrest." Reed wasn't unsympathetic to her demand. After all, Jonah probably had participated in a dirty deal to get land that belonged to the Native American community. Jerry might have helped him, too, but he couldn't arrest anyone without probable cause.

Since it was obvious that Ellie didn't intend to move, Reed met her eye-to-eye. "If and when I get proof, any proof, that Jonah's done something wrong, I'll arrest him. You have my word on that."

Ellie stared at him and then turned her dark eyes on Livvy. "Help us," she said, her voice still laced with anger. "This land deal has to be undone."

Livvy opened her mouth, looking as if she were about to say she was there to solve a murder, not get involved with community issues, but she must have rethought that because she nodded. "If I find anything, the sheriff will be the first to know."

That seemed to soothe Ellie enough to get her to move to the side, and Livvy and Reed continued up the steps to the county offices.

"How long has the protest been going on?" Livvy asked under her breath.

"On and off since the land deal over two years ago." And what Reed had said to Ellie hadn't been lip service. He would arrest Jonah if he could, and that arrest might go a long way to soothing the split that was happening in Comanche Creek.

He opened the door to the office building, and the cool air-conditioning spilled over him. Inside, there were some curious folks who eyed Livvy and him and then did some behind-the-hand whispers. Reed doled out some warning scowls and made his way down the hall. Jerry's office door was wide open, and he was seated at his desk, apparently waiting for them.

They stepped inside, and Reed shut the door. Not that they would have much privacy since the glass insert in the door allowed anyone and everyone to see in.

Livvy and he took the seats across from Jerry's desk. "Start talking," Reed insisted.

But Jerry didn't. Instead, he pulled out a manila file and slid it toward them. Reed opened it and saw that it was case notes from a murder that had happened over twenty years ago. The name on the file was Sandra Hutton.

Livvy's mother.

He aimed a raised eyebrow at Jerry and passed the file to Livvy. "What does this have to do with anything?" Reed asked.

"Sandra Hutton's killer has been hiding out in Mexico," Jerry explained with a tinge of smugness. "Maybe he's decided to return to Texas and create some havoc with Sandra's daughter. He could be the person who set fire to that cabin."

Livvy's reaction was slight. Just a small change in her breathing pattern. She moistened her lips, closed the file and tossed it back on Jerry's desk. "How did you get this information?" she asked.

"I requested it from the county sheriff's office. I told them it could be relevant to the investigation into the land deal that's got the Comanches so riled up."

In other words, Jerry had pulled strings so he could pry into Livvy's past.

"My mother's killer has no part in this," Livvy insisted.

"You're sure?" Jerry challenged.

"Positive."

Reed only hoped she was, but he'd do some checking when he got back to his office. For now though, he wanted answers and not a possible smokescreen.

"Were you at the cabin around the time Marcie was killed?" he asked Jerry.

There was no quick denial. Jerry studied Reed's expression and then nodded. "Why?"

"Because we found your tracks there." Reed studied Jerry as well, and the man certainly didn't seem particularly rattled by all of this. Of course, maybe that's because Jerry always seemed on edge about something. Like a pressure cooker ready to start spewing steam.

"I was at the cabin the morning of the murder." But then, Jerry hesitated. He had a pen in his hand, and he began rolling it between his fingers. "I got a call, telling me Marcie would be there, and I wanted to talk to her, to ask if she intended to go through with her testimony against Jonah Becker."

"And you," Livvy supplied. "Because if she'd testified against Jonah, you also would have been implicated."

Jerry bobbed his head, and rolled the pen faster. "At the time I put it together, I didn't know the land deal could be construed as illegal. I'm still not convinced it is. But I understand why the Native American community is upset. That's why they're protesting outside. I also understand they want someone to blame, but I wanted to make sure Marcie was going to get me a fair shake when she was on the witness stand."

"And did Marcie agree?" Reed asked.

"I didn't see her. She wasn't at the cabin when I got there so I left. That following morning, I heard about her murder. I swear, I had nothing to do with her death."

Reed wasn't sure he believed that. "So who called you to tell you about Marcie being at the cabin?"

This hesitation was a lot longer than the first, and the pen just started to fly over his fingers.

"Billy Whitley," Jerry finally said.

"Billy," Reed repeated, not that surprised but riled that he hadn't been given this information sooner. "How did he know Marcie was going to the cabin?"

Jerry picked up his phone. "I don't know, but you can ask him yourself." He pressed some numbers. "Billy, could you come over here a minute? Reed and the lady Ranger want to know why I was at the cabin that morning." He hung up. "He'll be here in a couple of minutes."

Reed wasn't going to wait for Billy to continue this

interrogation. "When Billy called to tell you about Marcie being at the cabin, you didn't ask him how he'd come by that information? Because Marcie hadn't exactly announced her whereabouts."

Jerry shook his head, tossed the pen on his desk and grabbed a Texas Longhorns mug near where the pen had landed. He gulped down enough coffee to choke himself. "I didn't ask. I was just thankful to finally have a chance to talk to her."

"And you're positive she wasn't there when you arrived?" Livvy asked.

"No sign of her. I didn't go in, but I looked in the windows. No one was in that cabin."

Livvy made a sound of disagreement. "She could have been hiding. I can't imagine that Marcie would have been happy to see her former boss, especially when she was scared to death of you."

Jerry couldn't and didn't deny that. It was common knowledge around town that Marcie had been afraid of him, so maybe she had indeed been wary enough to hide when she saw him skulking around the place.

"Did you happen to notice Shane while you were there?" Reed wanted to know.

"No." His answer was fast and prompted him to drink yet more coffee. "I told you, there was no one at that cabin."

Still, it was possible that both Shane and Marcie had come later. Jerry could be telling the truth.

Or not.

Reed wasn't ready to buy the man's story when Jerry had so much to lose from this situation.

There was a knock at the door, one sharp rap on the

glass insert, before it opened and Billy strolled in. "You wanted to see me," he said, aiming the not-too-friendly comment at Jerry. Charla was there, too, but she stood back in the doorway and didn't come in. "Charla and I were in the middle of eating lunch."

"I told them you were the one who called me about Marcie being at the cabin," Jerry volunteered.

"And we want to know how you came by that information," Reed added.

"I see." Billy pulled in a long weary breath and sat on the edge of Jerry's desk. "If you don't mind, I'd rather not divulge that information."

Reed stopped his mouth from dropping open, but that comment was a shocker. "I do mind." He got to his feet. "And if you don't tell me, I'll arrest you on the spot for obstruction of justice."

The usually friendly Billy suddenly didn't seem so friendly, and he tossed a glare at Jerry, probably because he wasn't pleased that the man had given Reed what Billy would have thought was private information.

Charla obviously ignored Billy's glare. "Ben Tolbert told Billy that Marcie was going to be at the cabin," the woman confessed.

Livvy and Reed exchanged glances, and he was certain neither was able to keep the surprise out of their eyes. "How did Ben know?"

Billy wearily shook his head and sighed. "He said he found out from Jeff Marquez."

Reed was very familiar with the name. Jeff Marquez was the EMT who'd helped Marcie fake her own death. "He's in county jail on obstruction of justice charges, and he won't be getting out anytime soon."

Billy nodded. "But he told Ben before he was arrested. Why, I don't know. Maybe Ben bribed him."

Ben didn't have the money for that, but Jonah sure did. Which brought them back full circle without eliminating any of the suspects. Jerry, Billy, Ben and Jonah all had the means, motives and opportunities to kill Marcie, but Reed was having a hard time believing that Ben would have allowed his son to take the blame for something he'd done.

That meant, he could focus more on the two men in the room, and the one rancher friend they had in common: Jonah. He wouldn't take Ben off his suspect list, but he did mentally move him to the bottom.

"I've done nothing illegal," Billy reiterated. "Neither has Jerry. And you're barking up the wrong tree, Reed. You already have the killer in custody."

"Maybe," Livvy mumbled. She got to her feet and stood next to Reed. Reed followed.

"Maybe?" Jerry challenged, and Reed didn't think it was his imagination that the man suddenly seemed very uncomfortable. Also, that wasn't a benign glance he aimed at Billy. And then Charla.

"Maybe," Livvy repeated, keeping a poker face. She walked out past Charla and into the hall.

Since there were lots of people milling around, too many, Reed didn't want to say anything that would be overheard and reported to Charla and the men. He waited until they were outside and away from the protestors.

"Smart move," he said under his breath, "to let them think you might have some evidence to prove Shane's innocence. And maybe their guilt."

"Well, I wanted to say something to shake them up a bit."

Mission accomplished. Now, they would have to wait to see who would react, and how, to the possibility that the charges against Shane weren't a done deal.

"I'm sorry Jerry brought up your mother," Reed told her.

"Not your fault. And this has nothing to do with her. That was an attempt to muddy the waters on his part. Makes you wonder just how deep he is into this. After all, other than Jonah, Jerry has the strongest motive because Marcie could have sent him to jail for years."

"Yeah, and he doesn't have Jonah's big bankroll to fight a long legal battle."

Livvy stayed quiet a moment. "So, of all our suspects who would be most likely to kill a woman and set up her former lover to take the blame?"

"Jerry," Reed said without hesitation. Still, that didn't mean Jonah or someone else hadn't put him up to it or even assisted. "While you're reexamining the gun, I want to talk to Shane again. Maybe he remembers something that'll help us unravel all of this."

He heard Livvy respond, but he didn't actually grasp what she said. That was because Reed saw something that got his complete attention.

The black rental car parked just up the street less than a block from his office.

"That's the vehicle that nearly ran me down," he told Livvy.

She put her hand over the butt of her service pistol. Reed did the same and tried to walk ahead of her so he could place himself between the car and her. Of course, Livvy wouldn't have any part of that. She fell in step beside him, and they made their way to the car.

"Can you see if anyone's inside?" she asked.

"No. The windows are too dark." And with the sunlight spewing in that direction, there was also a glare.

With each step they took, Reed's heart rate kicked up. It certainly couldn't be Billy, Charla or Jerry in that car since he'd just left them in Jerry's office, but it could be someone who'd been hired to intimidate Livvy and him.

Reed and Livvy were only a few yards away when the engine roared to life.

Livvy stopped and drew her weapon. Reed was about to push her out of harm's way, but it was already too late. The driver slammed on the accelerator, the tires squealing against the hot asphalt.

Reed cursed as the car sped past them. He cursed again when he got a glimpse of the driver.

This time it was Shane's father, Ben Tolbert.

Chapter Ten

Livvy stepped from the claw-footed tub and wrapped the thick terry-cloth towel around her. The hot bath had helped soothe some of her tight back and shoulder muscles, but it hadn't soothed her mind.

She dried off, slipped on her cotton nightgown and smeared her hand over the steam-coated mirror. A troubled face stared back at her, and she tried to assure herself that neither her career nor her personal life were in deep trouble.

But they were.

The Ranger captain had hit the roof when he learned about the destroyed crime scene, and it didn't help matters that she hadn't been able to confirm the arrest of their main suspect.

In fact, she'd done the opposite.

She'd created doubt with her questions about the murder weapon, and those doubts were fueling animosity between the Native American community and the rest of the town. According to the inn's owner, Betty Alice, there were whispers that Livvy was trying to clear Shane because of her personal involvement with Reed.

Maybe the new lab tests she'd ordered on the gun would help. Well, they might help clear Shane anyway, so they could concentrate on other suspects. But that wouldn't clear the rumors about Reed and her.

Worse, those rumors were partly true.

Other than that kiss, Reed and she hadn't acted on this crazy attraction, but that was no guarantee it wouldn't happen in the future.

And that was a sobering thought.

Despite all the problems a relationship with Reed would cause, she still wanted him. Bad. She wanted more than kisses. Livvy wanted sex.

No.

Sex wouldn't have been as unnerving as the fact that Livvy wanted Reed to make love to her. Something long, slow and very, very hot. And not a one-time shot, either. She was thinking of starting an affair with a lawman who could put some serious dents not just in her heart but in her professional reputation.

Cursing herself, Livvy brushed her teeth and reached for the door.

She heard it then.

A soft bump.

The sound had come from the bedroom.

Livvy turned to reach for her gun, only to realize she'd left it holstered on the nightstand. She hadn't wanted the gun in the steamy bathroom with all the moisture and humidity. Thankfully, she remembered she did have her cell phone with her though, because she had been concerned that she might not be able to hear it ring while the bathwater was running.

Of course, she'd locked the door to the room, and it

was entirely possible that Betty Alice had come up to bring her some towels or something. Still, with everything that'd happened, Livvy wished she had her gun.

She walked closer to the bathroom door, listening. And it didn't take long before she heard a second thump. Then, footsteps.

Someone was definitely in her room.

"Betty Alice?" she called out.

Nothing. The heavy footsteps stopped just outside the bathroom door.

Livvy grabbed her phone from the vanity, flipped it open but then hesitated. Calling Reed wasn't at the top of her list of things she wanted to do, but she might not have a choice.

"Who's out there?" she tried again.

No answer.

So, she waited, debating what she should do. She wasn't defenseless since she'd had some martial arts and hand-to-hand combat training, but she didn't want to go hand-to-hand with someone who was armed.

Like Marcie's killer.

The doorknob moved, and her heart dropped to her knees. This wasn't Betty Alice or even someone with friendly intentions, or the person would already have answered her.

There was another rattle of the doorknob, and then someone bashed against the door. That caused her heart to bash against her ribs. Oh, God. The door held, but Livvy knew she had no choice. She called Reed.

"This is Livvy. There's an intruder outside my door."

She didn't stay on the line. Livvy tossed the phone back onto the vanity so she could free her hands for a fight.

The person rammed against the door again, and she heard some mumbled profanity. She was almost positive it was a man's voice.

Another bash, and this time the wood cracked. It wouldn't hold up much longer, and she had to do something to improve her chances of survival if this turned into a full-fledged assault.

Livvy grabbed the scissors from her makeup bag and slapped off the lights. Since the lights were still on in her room, she hoped the intruder's eyes wouldn't have time to adjust to the darkness if he managed to get through that door.

Or rather *when* he got through.

The next bash sent the door flying open right at her, and Livvy jumped to the edge of the tub so she wouldn't get hit. Her heart was pounding. Her breathing was way too fast. And she had no hopes of being concealed in the dark room since her white nightgown would no doubt act as a beacon.

The man came at her.

Because the room was dark, Livvy couldn't see his face, but she caught his scent, a mixture of sweat and whiskey. He reached for her, but she swung the scissors at him and connected with his arm. She heard the sound of tearing fabric, and prayed she'd cut skin as well. He cursed in a raspy growling voice.

A voice she didn't recognize.

In the back of her mind, she was trying to identify this intruder. No. He was an assailant now, not merely an intruder, and with the profanity still hissing from his throat, he latched on to her hair and dragged her away from the tub. His grip was strong, and was obviously being fed with booze and adrenaline. Still, Livvy didn't just stand there and let him assault her.

Using the scissors again, she slashed at his midsection and followed it with a kick aimed at his shin. She missed. But he released the grip he had on her.

"Livvy?" someone shouted.

Reed.

She'd never been more thankful to hear someone call out her name. Better yet, he was nearby, and she could hear him barreling up the stairs. Her attacker must have heard Reed as well because he turned and raced out of the bathroom.

Livvy went after him.

Only the lamp was on, but she had no trouble seeing the man's back as he dove through the open window that led to the second-floor balcony.

"Livvy!" Reed shouted again.

He banged on the door, which was obviously still locked because the intruder hadn't entered that way. He'd apparently entered the same way he exited through the window. A window she was certain she'd locked as well because the balcony had steps that led down in the garden. She had known full well it was a weak security point.

Livvy hurried across the room to unlock the door, threw it open and faced a very concerned-looking Reed. "Are you okay?" There were beads of sweat on his face, and his breath was gusting.

Livvy didn't trust her voice. There'd be too much fear and emotion in it. Instead she pointed to the window where the evening breeze was billowing the pink curtains.

She dropped the scissors on the nightstand and grabbed her gun so she could go in pursuit, but Reed beat her to it.

He bolted through the window and started running.

REED RACED across the balcony, following the sounds of footsteps.

Unfortunately, whoever had broken into Livvy's room had a good head start, and Reed caught just a glimpse of the shadowy figure when he leaped off the bottom step and raced through the English-style country gardens that were thick with plants and shrubs.

There were too many places to hide.

And worse, too many ways to escape.

Reed barreled down the steps, but he no longer had a visual on the guy. Heck, he couldn't even hear footsteps on the grounds. Since finding him would be a crap shoot, Reed ran straight ahead because where the gardens ended there was a thick cluster of mature oaks. Beyond that was a greenbelt and then another street lined with businesses that would already be closed for the night. If the intruder was local, then he knew all he had to do was duck into one of the many alleys or other recesses.

And that was probably what had happened.

Because once Reed tore his way through the greenbelt and onto the street, he saw no one.

He stopped, listened and tried to hear any sound over the heartbeat that was pulsing in his ears.

Nothing.

Well, nothing except for his racing imagination. Maybe the escape had been a ruse. Maybe the guy was doubling back so he could have another go at Livvy. That put a knot in Reed's gut, and he whirled around and raced toward the inn.

A dozen scenarios went through his head. None were good. But he forced himself to remember that Livvy could take care of herself. Most of the time.

Tonight had obviously been the exception.

It might take a lifetime or two for Reed to forget the look of sheer terror he'd seen on her face when she'd unlocked the door to let him in.

He took out his cell phone and called his office so he could request backup. "Get any and all officers to Wade Street and the area back of the Bluebonnet Inn," he told the dispatcher. "We're looking for an unidentified male. About six feet tall. Dressed in black. Find him!" he ordered.

Reed didn't have to make it all the way back to the inn before he spotted Livvy. Dressed in her gown and bathrobe—and armed—she was making her way down the balcony stairs.

"Did you catch him?" she called out.

"No." And even from the twenty feet or so of distance between them, he saw her expression. The fear had been quickly replaced by anger.

Reed understood that emotion because he was well beyond the anger stage. He wanted to get the guy responsible for putting Livvy through this.

"Are you hurt?" he asked. He closed the distance between them and glanced around to make sure they weren't about to be ambushed.

"I'm fine," Livvy insisted.

But they both knew that was a lie. He caught onto

her arm to lead her back up the steps because he didn't want her out in the open.

"Betty Alice called a couple of minutes ago," Livvy explained. Her voice sounded calm enough. It was a cop's tone. Clinical, detached. She would have pulled it off, too, if he hadn't been touching her. Reed could feel her trembling. "She heard the noise and wanted to know what was going on. I told her to stay put and make sure all the windows and doors were locked."

"Good." He didn't want anyone in the path of his guy. Because it was entirely possible they weren't just dealing with an intruder but a killer.

Marcie's killer.

Reed led her back into her room, and closed the gaping window that had been used as the escape route. Because he didn't want anyone seeing their silhouettes, he turned off the lights as well.

"He broke through the bathroom door," Livvy explained. Her voice was soft now, practically a mumble, and she cleared her throat. "It was dark, and I couldn't see his face."

"But you're sure it was a man?"

"Positive. He smelled of sweat and liquor. And he had a strong grip." She rubbed her wrist. Even though she was a peace officer, that didn't make her bulletproof or spare her the emotion that came with an attack. Soon, very soon, the adrenaline would cause her to crash. "I'd left my gun in here so I couldn't get to it."

The fear in her voice was hard for Reed to hear, but he wouldn't be doing either of them any favors if he gave in to it. He had to have more answers if they hoped to catch this guy.

"Did he have a weapon?" Reed asked.

She hesitated a moment and then shook her head. "If he did, he didn't use it. He just grabbed me."

Now, that was odd. A killer, especially the one who'd shot Marcie, would likely have a gun. Or he could have grabbed Livvy's own weapon before going after her in the bathroom. But he hadn't.

Why?

Maybe this wasn't about harming Livvy but rather about scaring her. *Again.* If so, this SOB was persistent.

"I might have cut him with those scissors," Livvy added, tipping her head to where they lay on the night-stand. "I need to bag them."

"Later," Reed insisted. The scissors could wait.

She was shaking harder now, and Reed looped his arm around her and eased her down onto the bed so they were sitting on the edge. It wouldn't be long, maybe a few minutes, before he got an update from the deputies. If they got lucky, they might already have the attacker in custody. But just in case, Reed wanted to hear more.

"What about the possibility of transfer of DNA from him to you?" he asked.

"No," she answered immediately. "I wasn't able to scratch him, and other than his hand on my wrist, there was no physical contact."

Reed was thankful for that. Livvy hadn't been hurt. But the DNA proof would have been a good thing to have. Still, if she'd managed to cut him, that would give them the sample they needed.

"The door was locked," she continued, "but I guess he broke in through the window." Her voice cracked. The trembling got even worse.

And Reed gave up his fight to stay detached and impersonal. He pulled her even closer against him, until she was deep into his arms, and he brushed what he hoped was a comforting kiss on her forehead.

It didn't stay at the comfort level.

Livvy looked up at him, and even though the only illumination was coming from the outside security lights filtering through the curtains, he could clearly see her face. Yes, the fatigue and fear were there. But there was also an instant recognition that he was there, too, touching her.

Maybe it was just the adrenaline reaction, but Reed forgot all about that possibility when he lowered his head and kissed her.

There it was. That jolt. It slammed through him. So did her taste. After just one brief touch of their mouths, Reed knew he wanted more.

He slid his hand around the back of her neck so he could angle her head and deepen the kiss.

Yeah, it was stupid.

French-kissing his temporary partner and subordinate was a dumb-as-dirt kind of thing to do, but he also knew he had no plans to stop. He could justify that this was somehow easing Livvy's fear, but that was BS. This wasn't about fear. It was about this white-hot attraction that had flared between them since they first met.

Livvy didn't exactly cool things down, either. She latched on to him, bunching up his shirt in her fist, and she kissed him as if he were the cure to the trauma she'd just experienced.

And maybe he was.

Maybe they both needed this to make it through the next few minutes.

Her gown was thin. Reed quickly realized that when her chest landed against his. No bra. He could feel her breasts warm and soft against him. He felt even more of them when Livvy wound herself around him, leaning closer and closer until it was hard to tell where she started and he began.

Reed made it even closer.

He hauled her into his lap. Again, it was a bad idea. Really bad. But his body was having a hard time remembering why it was so bad because Livvy landed not just on his lap but with her legs straddling his hips.

The kisses continued. It was a fierce battle, and they got even more intense. So did the body contact. Specifically, her sex against his. And that was when Reed knew. This might have started as a kiss of comfort, but this was now down-and-dirty foreplay.

He made it even dirtier.

Reed slid his hand up her thigh, pushing up the flimsy gown along the way. She was all silk and heat, and the heat got hotter when he reached the juncture of her thighs. He paused a moment, to give Livvy a chance to stop things, but she only shoved her hips toward his hand.

And he touched her.

There was a lot more silk and heat here, and even though she was wearing panties, it wasn't much of a barrier. Part of him—okay, all of him—wanted to slide his fingers and another part of him into that slick heat. Only his brain was holding him back, and it just wasn't making a very good argument to convince the rest of him.

"This will have to be quick," she mumbled and took those wild kisses to his neck.

Quick sounded very appealing. Heck, any kind of sex with Livvy did. He wanted her. Worse, he wanted her now.

And that was why he had to stop.

She slid her hand over his erection and reached for the zipper on his jeans. However, Reed snagged her wrists. That didn't stop the other touching and, fighting him, she ground herself against his erection until he was seeing stars.

And having a boatload of doubts about stopping.

"Livvy," he managed to get out.

She finally stopped. Stared at him. Blinked. "You don't want to do this."

"Oh, I want it, and that's the understatement of the century. But you know what I'm going to say."

"The timing sucks." Her weary sigh shoved her breasts against his chest again.

He nodded and used every bit of willpower to ease her off his lap and back onto the bed. It didn't exactly end things. She landed with her legs slightly apart, and he got a glimpse of those barrier panties.

Oh, yeah. Definitely thin and lacy.

Reed had to clench his hands into fists to stop himself from going after her again.

"I'm sorry," she mumbled, shoving down her gown and scrambling away from him.

Hell. Now, she was embarrassed, and that was the last thing he wanted her to feel.

Even though it was a risk, Reed latched on to her shoulders and forced eye contact. "We will have sex," he promised. "It doesn't matter if it'll complicate the devil out of things, we'll land in bed. I'd just prefer if it happened when you weren't minutes off surviving an attack. I want to take my time with you. I want to be inside you not because you're scared but because you really want me inside you."

Her stare held, and for the briefest of moments, the corners of her mouth lifted into a smile. "I'm pretty sure the want was real. *Is* real," she corrected.

But Livvy waved him off, sighed again and scooped her hair away from her face. "I didn't think you'd be the sensible one."

He shrugged. "I don't feel too sensible. Actually, I'm damn uncomfortable right now."

They shared a smile, and because Reed thought they both could use it, he leaned over and kissed her. Not a foreplay kiss. But not a peck, either. He hoped it would serve as a reminder that this really wasn't over.

"Tonight's shot," he told her, pulling back. "We'll have reports to do. Maybe a suspect to interrogate. But tomorrow, why don't you plan on spending the night at my house?"

Her right eyebrow came up. "That'll get the gossips going."

"Yeah." It would. And it wouldn't be pretty. "I figure having you in my bed will be worth the gossip."

Livvy's eyebrow lifted higher. "You're sure about that?"

He was, but gossip was only part of it, and the look in her eyes indicated she understood that.

"I'm a Texas Ranger," she stated. "You're married to that badge, and this town. You don't have time to have an affair with me. Besides, judging from the way women around here look at you, you're the number-one catch. Husband and daddy material."

Reed couldn't disagree with any of it. He didn't consider himself a stud, but being single, male and employed did put him in big demand in a small town like Comanche Creek.

"What?" she questioned. "Did I hit a nerve?"

"No. I want marriage and kids someday," he admitted. Or at least he had at one time. Lately, however, those things seemed like a pipe dream. "What about you?"

But she didn't get a chance to answer. There was a knock at the door. "It's me, Kirby."

The sound of his deputy's voice sent them scurrying off the bed. "Did you find him?" Reed immediately asked.

"Not yet. But there's someone who wants to see you. He says it's important."

Livvy grabbed her clothes from the back of a chair and hurried into the bathroom. "I need to dress, but I won't be long," she assured him. Since the bathroom door was off its hinges, she got into the tub and pulled the shower curtain around her so she'd have some privacy. "And talk loud so I can hear what you're saying."

Reed unlocked the bedroom door, eased it open, and came face-to-face with someone he certainly hadn't expected to see.

Ben Tolbert.

Reed drew his weapon, surprising Kirby almost as much as he did their visitor.

Shane's father stared at the gun, then him. Actually, it was more of a glare with intense blue eyes that were a genetic copy of his son's. The dark brown hair was a match, too, though Ben's was threaded with gray.

"Did you come back to finish the job?" Reed asked.

"I don't know what you mean." He tipped his head to Reed's gun. "And is that necessary?"

"It is." Reed leaned in so he could get right in Ben's face. "Now, you're going to tell me why you've been harassing Sergeant Hutton."

"I haven't been," Ben insisted.

Reed had to hand it to him. It certainly didn't look as if Ben had just committed a B and E and then escaped on foot. However, Reed couldn't rule out that it was exactly what had happened.

"You want me to believe it's a coincidence that you're here tonight, less than thirty minutes after Sergeant Hutton was attacked?" Reed tried to keep the anger from his voice. He failed.

"Call it what you will. I didn't attack anyone, including that Texas Ranger. I'm just here to set the record straight."

Good. But Reed figured there would be a lot of lies mixed in with Ben's attempt to explain anything. First though, Reed looked at Kirby. "I'll handle this situation. Go ahead and help out the others by securing the place. I want the whole area checked for prints or any other evidence."

Kirby issued a "Will do," and headed down the stairs.

Reed heard the shower curtain rattle, and Ben's gaze flew right to Livvy. His snarl deepened. "So, there you are. I understand you're hell-bent on keeping my boy behind bars."

Livvy walked across the room and stood next to

Reed. "Actually, I'm hell-bent on examining the evidence. Too bad I keep getting interrupted." She paused just a heartbeat. "Did you try to kill me tonight?"

"I already answered that. No. Got no reason to go after you. *Yet.*"

That did it. Reed was already operating on a short fuse. He grabbed Ben with his left hand and slammed him against the doorjamb. "Threatening a peace officer's a crime, Ben. One I won't take lightly."

It took a moment for Ben to get his teeth unclenched. "I've done nothing wrong."

"What about burning down the cabin?" Reed challenged.

"I didn't do that." No hesitation. None. But Reed wasn't ready to believe him. Ben had one of the best motives for wanting Livvy out of town.

"In the woods near the cabin, we found a piece of a shirt that belongs to you," Livvy challenged.

"Yeah. I heard about that. Jonah said I bought it from a charity sale. Well, you know what? Jonah was lying, probably to save his own rich butt. But I'll be damned if I'll take the blame for something that man's done."

"So you're saying you're innocent?" Livvy clarified.

"Damn right I am."

Ben began a tirade of why he was being railroaded, but Reed was no longer paying attention to him. That was because he had spotted something.

Something that could blow this case wide open.

Reed latched on to Ben and got him moving toward the stairs. "Ben Tolbert, you're under arrest."

Chapter Eleven

Livvy gulped down more coffee and hoped the caffeine would help clear the fog in her head. The adrenaline from the attack had long since come and gone, leaving her with a bone-deep fatigue that was worse because she'd gotten only an hour or so of real sleep. That probably had something to do with the lumpy sofa in the sheriff's office break room that she'd used as a bed.

But it had more to do with Ben Tolbert's arrest.

God, was he really the one who'd attacked her? If so, Reed and she would soon know. The tiny rip on the sleeve of Ben's shirt had prompted his arrest.

A rip that she was thankful Reed had noticed.

She'd been too shaken from the attack to notice much of anything. So much for all her training. She'd reacted like a rookie, and it didn't really matter that she was one. She expected more of herself.

Livvy checked her watch again. It was 9:00 a.m. The start of the normal workday for most people, but Reed and she had been working this case most of the night. With luck, they would soon know if the small cut on Ben's shirt had been made with her nail scissors. Well, they'd know if the Ranger lab could match the fibers. Reed had had one of the deputies hand-deliver both Ben's shirt and the scissors, and any minute now, they should know if it was a match.

"I'm not releasing Ben Tolbert until I'm sure he's innocent," she heard Reed bark. He was no doubt still talking to Jerry Collier, the head of the land office and also Ben's newly hired attorney.

"Then schedule an arraignment," Jerry insisted. "I don't want you holding him without making it official."

"I'm doing us all a favor. It'll only create a mountain of paperwork if I officially arrest Ben."

"But you can release him until you get back that evidence." And Jerry continued to argue his client's case.

Livvy, however, shut out the conversation when her phone rang. It was the crime lab, but the number on the caller ID wasn't for trace and fibers, it was from the firearms section.

"Sergeant Hutton," she answered.

"It's me. Sam McElroy." This was someone she knew well. A firearms expert who'd been examining the weapon that had killed Marcie. But Livvy hadn't just sent him that particular gun. She had also couriered Sam the primary firearm that Shane used in the line of duty.

"You found something?" Livvy asked.

"I did. Your instincts were right. Someone tampered with the Rimfire pistol used to kill Marcie James."

Livvy let out the breath she'd been holding. She'd tried to stay objective, but because her feelings for Reed had softened to the point of melting, she'd automatically found herself rooting for his deputy. And, yes, that was a blow to her professionalism, but in the end, it was the truth that mattered anyway.

"The fingerprints were planted on the murder weapon," she said, stating a conclusion she'd already reached.

"Yes," Sam verified. "I compared the two firearms, and the grip pattern on the Rimfire is way off. There weren't enough pressure points to indicate Deputy Tolbert fired the gun, even though it was in his hand."

"Probably placed there by the real killer while the deputy was unconscious."

Shane had been set up, just as he said.

But by whom?

Had his father been the one to kill Marcie? Maybe. But why would he set up his son to take the fall? Still, he certainly wasn't the only suspect. Ben's attorney, Jerry, was on the short list. So was the mayor. Billy Whitley. And Jonah Becker.

"There's more," Sam continued. "I checked the lab, and one of the results was ready. I thought you'd like to know."

She listened as Sam explained the results of the sample she'd submitted after examining the cabin crime scene.

Livvy thanked Sam, ended the call and got up from the desk so she could give Reed the news, but the moment she saw his face, she knew he had news of his own.

"I'm getting my client out of jail," Jerry insisted. *"Now."* And with that, he stormed off.

Reed scrubbed his hand over his jaw, drank some coffee and then looked at her. "I just got a call from the lab. The fibers on your scissors didn't match Ben's shirt."

Her heart dropped to her stomach. "But what about the rip on the fabric?"

Reed lifted his shoulder. "It wasn't caused by the scissors."

Livvy forced herself to take a step back. "Ben could have changed his shirt after he attacked me."

"Yeah. He could have." But there was skepticism in Reed's voice.

Livvy shared that skepticism. Why would Ben have chosen to replace the shirt worn during the attack with one that was torn in such a way that it would only cast more suspicion on him?

"I have to let him go," Reed said. "As soon as Jerry and he sign the papers, he'll be out. But I'll keep an eye on him. And I'll take some measures to make sure you're safe."

She remembered his invitation when they'd kissed in her room. "You want me to stay at your place?"

"Yes." More skepticism. "I know what you're thinking. It'll set tongues wagging, but I'd planned on spending more time with you anyway whether that was at work or the inn. This just makes it easier for me to keep you safe because I'm not going to let Ben or anyone else have a go at you."

Livvy wanted to object. She wanted to remind him that she could take care of herself. But she wasn't stupid. And she didn't want to die.

"I have news, too." It seemed a really good time to change the subject. "The fingerprint pattern on the murder weapon doesn't match the one on Shane's service pistol."

She saw the fatigue drain from Reed's face. "You mean he's innocent."

She nodded. "That's what the evidence indicates."

So why was she so reluctant to declare that Shane wasn't a killer?

All the pieces fit for him to have been set up. It was also obvious that someone else was out there, someone who wanted to stop them from learning the truth. Shane certainly hadn't been responsible for those attacks because he had been behind bars when they occurred. But Livvy couldn't totally dismiss the possibility that perhaps Shane was the mastermind who'd set all of this in motion.

Still, there were others with more powerful motives than love gone wrong.

"The firearms expert who called me about the gun also had the results from one of the lab tests," she continued. "The blood spatter we found in the cabin was consistent with the head injury that Shane described. And it was his blood."

Now there was relief in his eyes. Reed looked as if he were about to shout in victory, but his mood changed again.

Did he have doubts as well?

"Thank you," he said.

He reached out and almost idly ran his fingers through the ends of her ponytail. It was the gesture of a man comfortable with touching her. A gesture that shocked Livvy but not nearly as much as her own reaction did. She moved in to the touch, letting his thumb brush against her cheek.

It was intimate.

And wrong.

As usual, the timing was awful. They were both exhausted. Both had a dozen things to do that were important and related to the job. But it was as if those deeply seeded primal urges just weren't going to leave them alone.

"You know, I'll be leaving as soon as we've wrapped up this case," Livvy said. Not that she needed to remind him or herself of that.

"I know." And he seemed genuinely disappointed. "But Austin's not that far from here. Less than an hour away."

Far enough, she silently added.

If she stopped this now…but then she halted that particular thought because it was useless.

She couldn't stop this now.

It was only a matter of time before they landed in bed, and her hope was that this heat between them would be so intense that it would quickly burn itself out and Reed and she could get back to normal.

Reed drew in a hard breath, pulled back his hand and turned. "I need to do the paperwork for Shane's release." Then, he paused. "You're sure he's innocent?"

"No," she admitted. "But the evidence doesn't point to him being guilty."

Reed nodded and walked away, leaving Livvy to wonder if she'd just given a killer a get-out-of-jail-free card.

The phone on Reed's desk rang, and Livvy glanced out into the reception area to see if Eileen was there to answer it. She wasn't, so Livvy took the call.

"It's me, Ben Tolbert," the caller said.

Livvy tried to keep the strain out of her voice. "Are you already out of jail?"

"Yeah, as of thirty seconds ago."

Her heart suddenly felt very heavy. "Where are you?"

"I'm going nowhere near you. Where's Reed?"

"Busy. I'm surprised you didn't see him because he was headed to the jail." She'd let Shane be the one to tell his father that he'd been cleared of the murder charges.

"I musta missed him. I didn't exactly hang around the place after I told my boy I'd be gettin' him out of that cell soon enough."

Sooner than Ben thought. "I don't expect Reed back for ten or fifteen minutes, but I can take a message."

Silence. Several long seconds of it. "Tell him I've been doing some digging."

Livvy had to get her teeth apart so she could speak. "We don't want you to interfere in this case."

"Well, somebody has to. You got the wrong man in jail, and I intend to do everything I can to prove it. So, consider this a tip. I heard from a reliable source that Billy Whitley faked historical documents that allowed Jonah Becker to buy that land—the land that's causing all the ruckus with the Comanches."

Billy Whitley, another suspect. "Why would Billy have done that?"

"Money, what else? Jonah paid him to do it. Jonah's too smart to make a payment that could be traced back to him, but there will be a trail all right. You're just gonna have to hunt hard and find it."

Maybe. If this was a legit lead. "Who's your reliable source?"

"Can't tell you that."

"Then why should I believe you?" Livvy pressed. "You might be saying all of this to take suspicion off yourself."

"No reason for that. I haven't done anything wrong."

The attack came racing back at her. The man's scent.

The rasp of his breathing. How he'd come at her. She'd been lucky not to have been hurt. Or worse.

"I think Billy's the one who set up my boy," Ben continued, and that accusation immediately grabbed her attention.

"Why do you think that?"

"Because if Billy did fake those documents, then he's as much of a suspect as Jonah."

"And your lawyer," Livvy pointed out. "Jerry has motive, too."

"A lot of people have motive," Ben admitted, "but I'm betting Billy or his wife is responsible for this."

Yes, Charla could have been in on it. "Again, do you have proof?"

There was another hesitation, longer than the first. "What's the fax number there?" he asked.

Surprised by his request, Livvy looked at the machine and read the fax number that she located on the top of it. "Why do you need it?"

"Because I'm about to send you something. Consider it a gift."

Livvy didn't really want any gift from a suspected killer, but it didn't take long before the machine began to spit out a faxed copy.

"The first page is a copy of the way the deed was filed decades ago," Ben explained. "Look at line eight. When you get the second page, you'll see how it was changed. It no longer says 'the Comanche people.' It lists ownership as none other than Billy and Charla Whitley."

Livvy didn't say a word until both documents had finished printing, and her attention went to line eight on the pages.

There had indeed been a change.

"How did you get these?" she demanded.

"I can't tell you that."

"You stole them," Livvy accused. Then, she cursed under her breath. "And if you did, that means we can't use them as evidence. We wouldn't be able to prove that you're not the one who did the tampering."

His silence let her know that Ben was considering that. "What if I swear on my son's life that those papers are real?"

"That won't stand up in court." But it did in some small way convince her that Ben might be telling the truth, about this anyway. Livvy decided to put him to the test. "Shane will be out of jail soon. It appears someone planted his prints on the murder weapon."

"Are you sure?" Ben snapped.

"Sure enough for Reed to be processing his release as we speak."

Ben paused. "Is this some kind of trick? It is, isn't it? You're just telling me what I want to hear. You want to hang my boy."

"I want to hang the person responsible for Marcie's murder," Livvy clarified. "And if that had turned out to be Shane, he'd still be in jail. That's true for any future evidence we might find. But for now, the evidence isn't enough for us to hold your son."

Ben mumbled something. "Guess that means you're still gunning for him."

Livvy huffed. "Only if Shane's guilty of something. Is he?"

"I knew it." Ben cursed again. "I knew you'd still go after my boy."

Livvy didn't even bother to repeat that she wasn't on some vendetta to convict Shane of anything. But Ben might have a vendetta of his own.

"Did you tamper with these documents to implicate Billy so you could get your son cleared of murder charges?" Livvy asked.

"No. The documents are real, and Billy changed them so Jonah could buy that land."

His answer was so fast and assured that it surprised Livvy. Ben could have taken the easy way out. Heck, he could have hung up the phone and raced to the jail to see Shane.

But he hadn't.

Instead, Ben had stuck to his story about Billy's involvement.

Livvy looked at the documents again. They certainly seemed real, and that meant she had to call Reed.

They needed a search warrant ASAP.

"My advice?" Ben said. "Be careful, Sergeant Hutton. Because once everyone in town knows what Billy and Jonah did, somebody's gonna get hurt. Bad."

Livvy didn't question the threat because she knew Ben was right. The town was already on the verge of an explosion, and this certainly wouldn't help.

"One more thing," Ben added. "Everything we've said here, somebody's probably overheard. Somebody who's probably running to tell Billy to destroy anything that might put these murders on him. He'll be desperate. Real desperate. If I was you, I'd get over there right now."

Livvy didn't argue or disagree. She dropped the phone back onto its cradle and hurried to find Reed.

Chapter Twelve

Reed replayed everything Livvy had told him about her conversation with Ben. In fact, Reed had spent a good deal of the day replaying it and trying to figure out what the devil was going on.

He wasn't any closer to the answer than he had been when the day started.

Thankfully, Woody had come back from his fishing trip. Well, he had after Reed had sent his deputy out to tell the man what had been going on in town. Woody had returned immediately, just in time to give Reed permission to search Billy's office in the city building.

Reed had personally gone through every inch of Billy's office. Nothing was out of order, nor were there any signs of tampered documents. It'd helped that Billy hadn't been there during the search, but he would find out about it. That was a given, even though Reed had sworn Billy's secretary to secrecy.

Besides, there was a bigger secret that Reed had to unravel.

Shane was out of jail now. Cleared because of

planted evidence that Livvy had discovered. So, that meant there was a killer out there who had to be caught.

Reed just wasn't sure this was the way to go about doing it.

Beside him on the seat of his truck, Livvy was napping. Thank God. She was the only person in town who in the past twenty-four hours had had less sleep than him. Of course, she hadn't wanted the nap. In fact, she'd fought it like crazy, but in the end, the boring stakeout of Billy's house had been too much for the fatigue, and she was now asleep with her head dropped onto his shoulder.

Reed didn't mind the close contact with her rhythmic breath brushing against his neck. He didn't even mind that her left breast was squished against his arm. The touching was a surefire way of remembering that she was a woman, and that in turn was a surefire way of keeping him awake.

Shifting a little so that his arm wouldn't go numb, Reed checked their surroundings again. It was dark now, still hotter than hell, and no one had come or gone from the Whitley house in the entire three hours that Livvy and he had been keeping watch. The area wasn't exactly brimming with activity since it was located just outside the city limits and a good half mile from any neighbors.

Reed had called Billy earlier, before he'd even gone to the man's office to search. Billy had been home then. Sick with a sudden case of the stomach flu, he'd said, and he had a doctor's appointment in San Antonio and wouldn't be home until later in the evening. Then, he'd hung up and hadn't answered the phone when Reed tried to call him again. That'd sent Livvy and Reed out to Billy's place because they didn't want the man to try to destroy any evidence.

But where were Billy and Charla now? Still at the doctor's office or perhaps pretending to be there?

And had someone already tipped him off about Ben somehow finding the doctored land record? Or the office search? Maybe. But if Billy did know, the last thing Reed expected the man to do was go on the run.

Well, unless Billy really was a killer.

Reed checked his cell phone again. Nope. He hadn't missed a call. Not that he thought he had since the phone was set to a loud ring. That meant Kirby hadn't succeeded in getting the search warrant yet. Reed hadn't needed one for a municipal office because Woody had given him permission to search. But he'd need one for a private residence.

He'd get it, too.

There was no way a judge would turn it down with the evidence of the doctored documents, but Comanche Creek wasn't exactly flooded with judges, and Kirby had gotten stuck driving all the way over to Bandana, a good hour away, just to find Judge Calder, who was visiting relatives.

Reed had considered just going in and looking around Billy and Charla's place. But that wouldn't be smart if Livvy and he managed to find something incriminating. If Billy was the killer, Reed didn't want anything like an unlawful search to stand in the way of the man's arrest and conviction. Of course, Reed had considered that this could be an exigent circumstance, where a peace officer could conduct a search without a warrant if there was a likelihood that evidence might be destroyed, but again, he didn't want that challenged. He wanted to follow the letter of the law on this one.

Livvy stirred, her breath shivering as if she were in the throes of a bad dream. But Reed rethought that theory when her eyes sprang open and her gaze snapped to his.

Even though the only illumination came from the hunter's moon and the yellow security light mounted at the end of the drive, he could clearly see her expression. No nightmare. But no doubt disturbing.

This dream was perhaps of the sexual variety.

Or maybe that was wishful thinking on his part. His thoughts were certainly straying toward that variety when it came to Livvy.

"You shouldn't have let me fall asleep," she mumbled and eased her breast away from his arm.

Maybe it was his surly mood, or even his own fatigue, but Reed put his hand around the back of her neck, hauled her to him and kissed her.

He got proof of the direction of her thoughts when she didn't resist. She kissed him right back.

And more.

Livvy caught onto his shoulders and adjusted their positions so that he got more of that breast contact. Both of them. He'd been hot before, but that kicked up the heat even more.

The kiss continued. Deepened. So did the body contact. They were both damp with sweat, and with the moisture from the kiss, everything suddenly felt right for sex.

It wasn't, of course.

And because they were literally sitting in his truck in front of a suspected killer's house, Reed remembered that this was not a safe time to engage in an oral rodeo with a woman he wanted more than his next breath.

He pulled back. Man, his body protested. But before his body could come up with a convincing argument as to why this could continue, Reed moved Livvy back onto the seat so that they were no longer touching.

"I feel like I'm back in high school," she complained.

Not Reed. In high school his willpower had sucked, and he wouldn't have let something like common sense or danger get in the way of having sex.

And if he wasn't careful, he wouldn't let those things get in the way now.

His phone rang, slicing through the uncomfortable silence that followed Livvy's confession. Reed wasn't pleased with the interruption, but he was damn happy about getting this call.

"Kirby," Reed answered. "Tell me you have a search warrant."

"I got it. The judge didn't put any limits on it, either. You can go through the house, grounds and any out-buildings or vehicles. You still waiting at Billy's house?"

"Yeah. Bring the warrant to us."

"Will do. I'll be there in about forty-five minutes."

Reed hung up, knowing he wouldn't wait that long. The warrant had been issued and that was enough. "Let's go," he instructed.

Livvy immediately grabbed her equipment bag, got out and joined him as they walked toward the front of the house. "You plan to bash down the door?" she asked.

"No need." Reed lifted the fake rock to the left side of the porch and extracted a key.

"That's not very safe," she commented.

No, but until recently most people around Comanche Creek hadn't had cause to be concerned about safety.

Reed unlocked the door and stepped inside. "Anyone home?" he called out just to be sure that Billy or his wife weren't hiding out. But he got no answer.

He was thankful that the house wasn't huge and also that he had been there often enough to know the layout. "Billy's office is this way," he said, leading Livvy down the hall that was off the living room. "His wife, Charla, is somewhat of a neat freak so if he brought the land documents home, they'd be in here."

They went into the office, turned on the lights and immediately got to work. The room wasn't large, but it was jammed with furniture, including a desk that held a stack of papers, folders and an open laptop. Reed went there first, and Livvy headed to a filing cabinet.

"What are some possible file names that would be red flags?" she asked.

"Anything that deals with Native American land. Or something called the Reston Act. That's the name of the old law that gave the Comanches the land."

Livvy took out some latex gloves from her bag, put them on and tossed him a pair. She then pulled open the drawer. "So, if that law is on the books, why wasn't the land deal challenged when it happened two years ago?"

"It was, by the activist Native American group. But then Billy produced this document that supposedly superseded the Reston Act. It seemed legit, and there were other documents on file to back it up. Basically, those documents claimed that the land had only been leased to the Comanches and that ownership reverted to the original owner, who was Jonah's great-great-grand-father."

"Convenient," Livvy mumbled.

"Maybe." Reed put on the gloves and thumbed through the papers and files. "Or maybe someone doctored that, too. The activist group didn't have the funds to fight a long legal battle, so they turned to Marcie. They wanted her to testify that at Jonah's urging, Jerry Collier orchestrated the illegal land deal."

"And we know what happened to Marcie." Livvy paused, and he heard her rifling through the files. "Other than Billy, who else could have faked the documents?"

Reed figured she wouldn't like the answer. He certainly didn't. "Anyone with access to the land office."

Woody, Billy, Jerry and, yes, even Jonah. Basically, anyone with enough motive and determination could have figured out a way to get into those files since security was practically nonexistent.

That had changed. Since the murders, Reed had insisted the city council install a better security system, one with surveillance cameras. But this crime—the altered documents—had happened long before the murders.

"I might have something," Livvy said.

But when he looked at her, she no longer had her attention on the files. She was studying something in the bookcase behind the cabinet. "There are two books here, one on Comanche burial rituals and another on local Native American artifacts."

That grabbed his attention, especially the one about rituals. Reed pulled it from the shelf, went straight to the index and saw the references for the red paint and ochre clay used in burials. It was critical because two dead bodies found the previous week had been prepared with red paint and clay.

"Hell," Reed mumbled. He continued to thumb through the book and noticed the pages with the clay references had been dog-eared.

Of course, Billy's wife was Native American. Maybe the books were hers. But Reed suspected if they had been, they wouldn't be in Billy's office. "It's circumstantial, but we can still use it to build a case. If Billy's guilty," he added.

"I think we might have something more than just circumstantial," Livvy corrected.

Reed looked up from the book. Livvy was photographing the trash can. She took several pictures and then carefully pushed aside some wadded-up paper and pulled out a latex glove, one very similar to the pair she was wearing.

"Any reason Billy would need this in his office?" she asked.

"None that I can think of." Especially none that involved anything legal.

Livvy eased the glove right side out and examined it. "We might be able to get DNA from the inside," she explained.

She placed the glove back on top of the paper wads, took the spray bottle of Luminol from her bag. She put just a fine mist on a small area that would cover the back of the hand.

It lit up.

An eerie blue glow.

Indicating there was blood.

Reed cursed again. "Is there enough for a DNA match to Marcie's blood?"

"All it takes is a tiny amount." She leaned in closer. "There's a smudge. It could be gunshot residue. Let's go ahead and bag this, and I'll bring the entire trash can in case the other glove is down in there."

Reed took one of the evidence bags to encase the glove while Livvy clicked off more photographs. The trash can and the glove would be sent to the lab that would have the final word on any biological or trace evidence, but it wasn't looking good for Billy.

Was Billy really a killer?

Reed had to admit it was possible. He'd known Billy all his life and had never seen any indication that the man was violent. Still, he'd also seen desperate people do desperate things, and Billy might have been desperate to cover his tracks and therefore kill Marcie.

"Once Kirby gets here with the warrant, I'll have him lock down the place so we can have time to go through everything else," Reed explained.

It also might be a good idea for them to drive the glove and trash can to the lab themselves. If they could get a quick match to Marcie on the blood, then Reed would arrest Billy.

"Are you okay?" Livvy asked.

Reed realized then that he was staring at the bagged glove with what had to be an expression of gloom and doom on his face. "I was just hoping the killer was someone else. Someone I didn't know."

"I understand." She touched his arm with her fingertips. A gesture no doubt meant to soothe him.

And it might have worked, too, if there hadn't been a sound. A slight rustling from outside the house.

"Probably the wind," Livvy said under her breath.

"Probably." But Reed set the bagged glove aside in case he had to reach for his gun. "It's not Kirby. We would have heard the cruiser drive up." Besides, it was too soon for the deputy to have arrived.

There was another sound. One that Reed couldn't quite distinguish, but it had come from the same direction as the first.

"I'll have a look," he insisted, and drew his weapon.

Livvy put down the trash can and did the same. "You think Billy's out there?" she whispered.

Someone certainly was—Reed was positive of that when he heard the next sound.

Footsteps, just outside the window.

He turned, aiming his gun.

Just as the lights went out and plunged them into total darkness.

Reed saw the shadow outside the window and reached for Livvy to get her out of the way. But he was a split second too late.

The bullet tore through the glass and came right at them.

Chapter Thirteen

Livvy heard the shot, but she wasn't able to see who had fired at them. That was because Reed shoved her to the floor. She landed, hard, and the impact with the rustic wood planks nearly knocked the breath out of her.

Thankfully, Reed didn't have any trouble reacting.

He rolled to the side, came up on one knee, and using the desk as cover, he took aim. She couldn't see him clearly, but she heard the result. His shot blasted through what was left of the glass on the far right window.

"Who's out there?" she whispered, getting herself into position so she could fire as well.

"I can't tell."

Well, it was obviously someone who wanted them dead.

That hadn't been a warning shot. It'd come much too close to hitting them. And worse, it wasn't over. Reed and she were literally pinned down in a room with three large windows, any one of which could be an attack point. But it wasn't the only way a gunman could get to them.

There was a door behind them.

Livvy rolled onto her back so she could kick it shut.

At least this way the culprit wouldn't be able to sneak up on them. And that led her to the big question.

Who exactly was the culprit?

"Billy Whitley," Livvy mumbled under her breath. Livvy scrambled to the side of the desk as well.

Another shot came through the window. Not from Reed this time. But from their attacker. Reed immediately returned fire, but Livvy held back and tried to peer over the desk and into the night. She hoped to get a glimpse of the shooter's location, but the only thing she saw was the darkness.

The next shot tore through the oak desk and sent a spray of splinters right at them. Reed shoved her back to the floor, and she caught onto his arm to make sure he came down as well.

More shots.

One right behind the other.

Livvy counted six, each one of the bullets slamming into the desk and the wall behind them. A picture fell and smashed on the floor next to her feet. The crash blended with the sounds of the attack. The chaos. And with her own heartbeat that was pounding in her ears.

Then, the shooting stopped.

Livvy waited, listening, hoping the attack was over but knowing it probably wasn't.

"He's reloading," she mumbled.

"Yeah." Reed glanced over at her. "How much ammunition do you have on you?"

"A full magazine in the gun and a backup clip. You?"

"Just what I have here. The rest is in the truck."

The truck parked outside where the shooter was.

Livvy didn't need to do the math. She knew. Reed

and she wouldn't be able to go bullet-to-bullet with this guy because he probably had brought lots of backup ammunition with him. However, that was only one of their problems.

There was Kirby to consider.

The deputy would arrive soon, maybe in twenty minutes or less. The shooter might gun him down if Reed and she didn't warn him.

"I have to call Kirby," Livvy let him know.

Reed kept his attention nailed to the windows and passed her his phone. "Request backup, too, but don't have them storming in here. Tell him to keep everyone at a distance until they hear from me. But I do want lights and sirens. I want this SOB to know he's not going to escape."

Livvy agreed and made the call. She'd barely got out the warning when the shots started again. Obviously, the gunman had reloaded, and he began to empty that fresh ammunition into the room. He was literally tearing it apart, and that included the desk. It wouldn't be long before the shots destroyed the very piece of furniture they were using as cover.

"Kirby's calling backup," she relayed to Reed and tossed the phone back to him.

"The shots are getting closer."

Because of the noise, it took a moment for that to sink in. Livvy's gaze whipped in the direction of the windows again, and she listened.

God, Reed was right. The shots were getting closer, and that meant the shooter was closing in on them. If he made it all the way to the windows, he'd have a much better chance of killing them.

"He knows we don't have enough ammunition to hold him back," Reed explained. "We have to get out of this room."

Livvy didn't have any doubts about that. But what she did doubt was they'd be able to escape without being shot. The gunman might already be at the windows.

Of course, Reed and she could fire right back.

And they would. Until they were out of bullets. After that, well, they'd still fight. Livvy had no intentions of letting this goon get away, and Reed no doubt felt the same.

With the shots still knifing all around them, Livvy crawled to the door and reached for the knob.

"Be careful," Reed warned. "He might not be alone out there."

Mercy. She should have already thought of that. If this was Billy firing those shots, then he could be working with his wife. Charla could be in the house. Not that there had been any signs of that, but it was something Livvy had to prepare herself to face.

She aimed her gun and used her left hand to open the door. Just a fraction. She peered out into the hall. Thankfully, her eyes had adjusted to the darkness so even though the lights were off, she didn't see anyone lurking outside the doorway.

"It's clear," she relayed to Reed.

That got him moving. With his back to her and his attention still on the windows, he made his way to her and fired a glance into the hall.

"I'll go first, and you come out right behind me," Reed explained over the thick, loud blasts. "Stay low, as close to the floor as possible. You cover the right side of the hall. I'll cover the left."

Livvy's heart sank lower because the shots were even closer now.

Reed came up a little and fired a bullet in the direction of those shots. He didn't even aim, because it was meant to get the guy to back off. It might buy them a second or two of time, but that was all they needed.

Livvy didn't bother with the equipment bag. It was too big and bulky to take with them. She only hoped that it would still be there at the end of this attack. Just in case it wasn't, she snatched the bagged glove and shoved it into the waist of her jeans.

"Now!" Reed ordered.

Livvy didn't waste any more time. She scrambled to the side so Reed could get by her. He practically dove into the hall but as he'd instructed, he stayed on the floor. Livvy did the same, and she landed out in the darkness with her back to his.

She had the easy end of the hall to cover. Only one room that was directly at the end. Probably a bedroom. And the door was closed. However, that didn't mean the shooter wouldn't go through one of the room's windows to get to them and try to stop their escape.

"I don't see anyone," she reported.

"Neither do I."

Livvy didn't exactly breathe easier because that side contained all the main living areas. There were multiple points of entry, and if the gunman was indeed Billy, he would know the way to get in that would cause the biggest threat to Reed and her.

"This way," Reed instructed.

He remained crouched, with his gun aimed and ready, and he began to inch his way toward the front of the house where they'd entered. Livvy did the same while keeping watch on the bedroom. She didn't want anyone blasting through that door.

Then, again, the shots stopped.

Reed and she froze, and Livvy tried to steady her heartbeat so she could listen. But the only thing she heard was their breathing.

"Let's move," Reed insisted.

Yes, because they were still in the line of sight of the office windows, and Livvy couldn't risk reaching up to close the door. The last thing they wanted was for the shooter to have a visual on them.

Reed began to move again, and Livvy followed. She kept watch on both the office and the bedroom door, but there were no sounds coming from either.

Mercy.

Where was the shooter?

She doubted he'd just give up. No. He was looking for a place to launch another attack.

Reed stopped again when they got to the end of the hall, and she glanced at him as he peered out into the living room. It was just a quick look, and then he whipped his attention to the other side, to the kitchen. He didn't say anything, didn't make a sound, but Livvy figured he didn't see anyone or else he would have taken aim.

She heard it then. The knob on the kitchen door rattled. Reed and she both shifted in that direction, but she continued to watch the bedroom and now the office.

Another rattle. Someone was obviously trying to get

in, but the door was apparently locked because the third try wasn't just a rattle. Someone gave it a frantic, violent shake.

Livvy had just enough time to wonder why Billy hadn't just used his key to gain entry when she heard another sound.

A siren.

Kirby or one of the backup deputies had finally arrived. Or would soon. Reed and she wouldn't have to hold out much longer.

But that brought a new concern. A new *fear*.

The gunman might get away.

That couldn't happen. Reed and she couldn't continue to go through this. They had to catch the killer and get him off the streets. If not, this wouldn't stop.

Reed obviously had the same concern because he moved out of the hall so he'd be in a better position if the gunman did indeed come through the kitchen door. The siren might scare him off.

Or not.

The *or not* was confirmed when someone kicked at the door. Hard. And then it sounded as if someone was ramming against it.

Livvy considered shooting at the door. Reed likely did, too, but this might not be the gunman. It could be Charla who was trying to get away from her now deranged husband. Or maybe it was someone from backup responding.

"This is Sheriff Hardin," Reed called out. "Who's out there?"

Nothing. And the attempts to get inside stopped.

Livvy couldn't hear if the person moved away

because the sirens drowned out any sound the person might have made.

Reed cursed and scurried to the snack bar area that divided the living room from the kitchen. He kept his aim and focus on the door while Livvy tried to keep watch all around them.

"Call Kirby." Reed tossed her his phone again. "Make sure he's locking down the area."

But it might be too late. The killer could already be on the move and escaping.

"Smoke," she heard Reed say.

She lifted her head, pulled in a long breath, and cursed. Yes, it was smoke, and she figured it was too much to hope that it was coming from some innocent source.

Livvy pressed Redial, and Kirby answered on the first ring. She relayed Reed's message and told the deputy to await further orders. She'd barely managed to say that before there was another shot.

This one, however, hadn't been fired into the house. It'd come from outside but in the direction of the driveway.

Reed and she waited for several long seconds. Breaths held. With her pulse and adrenaline pounding out of control. Livvy didn't take her eyes off the bedroom just up the hall, and she was primed and wired for an attack when the cell phone rang.

The unexpected sound caused her to gasp, and she glanced down at the lit screen. It was Kirby.

"There's a fire on the back porch," Kirby shouted. "You need to get out of there."

Maybe Reed heard the deputy because he motioned for her to move toward the front door.

"Do you see the shooter?" Livvy asked Kirby.

"I think so. He's on the west end of the house."

By the driveway, just as she'd expected. "Is he trying to get in?"

"No. He's just sitting there, leaning against the wall."

Sitting? Or maybe crouching and waiting? "Can you see who it is?"

"No," Kirby quickly answered. "I'm using my hunting binoculars. They have night vision, and I'm getting a pretty close look, but he has a hat covering his face."

So if it was Billy, he could be trying to conceal his identity. "How bad is the fire?" The smoke was starting to billow into the living room.

"Not bad right now, but I wouldn't stay in there much longer. Uh, Sergeant Hutton?" Kirby continued. "I think the guy's been shot. He's got his hand clutched to his chest, and his gun is on the ground beside him."

Shot? It was possible. Reed and she had fired several times, and any one of the bullets could have hit the gunman.

"The shooter might be wounded," she told Reed. "He's by the driveway."

Reed didn't say anything for several seconds. "Tell Kirby to cover us. We're going out there."

Livvy told Kirby their plan while they were on the move toward the front door. Reed opened it.

Nothing.

Certainly there was no gunman waiting just outside.

Reed went first, and Livvy followed him. As they'd done inside, they moved back to back so they could cover all sides. At the end of the road, she saw Kirby standing next to a cruiser. Covering them. She hoped they wouldn't need it.

The night was sticky and hot, and the smoke was already tainting the air. Livvy heard the high, piercing buzzing of mosquitoes that immediately zoomed in on them.

Reed batted the mosquitoes away and hurried to the back of the house. He paused only a few seconds to check the area where the last shot had been fired.

Then, Reed took aim.

And fired.

Livvy tried to scramble to get into position so she could assist, but Reed latched on to her arm and held her at bay. "I fired a warning shot," he told her. "The guy didn't move an inch."

Which could mean the gunman was perhaps too injured to react. Or this could be a trick to lure them out into the open so he could kill them.

"Cover me," Reed insisted.

He stood, braced his wrist for a better aim and started toward the shooter.

Livvy eased out so she could fire if necessary. She saw the shooter then. Dressed in what appeared to be jeans, a dark shirt and a baseball cap that covered his face. His back was against the exterior of the house. His handgun on the ground beside him.

The guy certainly wasn't moving.

Reed inched closer. So did Livvy. And thanks to the moonlight she saw the man did indeed have his left hand resting on his chest.

She also saw the blood.

Ahead of her, Reed stooped and put his fingers

against the man's neck. Livvy waited and didn't lower her guard just in case this was a ploy.

"He's dead," Reed relayed.

"Dead," Livvy repeated under her breath.

She walked closer and stared down at the body. Though she was more than happy that this guy wasn't still taking shots at them, it sickened her a little to realize that she might have been the one to kill him.

Reed reached down with his left hand and eased the cap away from the man's face.

Livvy's stomach roiled.

It was Billy Whitley.

"We have to move the body," she heard Reed say, and he reached for Billy's feet. "The fire's spreading fast."

Livvy took hold of Billy as well and glanced at the flames that were eating their way through the back of the house. Reed was right—they didn't have much time. The fire had swelled to the wood-shake roof, and there were already tiny embers falling down around them.

They had dragged the body a few yards when she saw something fall out of the pocket of Billy's jeans.

A piece of paper.

Since she was still wearing a latex glove, she reached for it, but reaching was all she managed to do. The cabin seemed to groan, the sound echoing through the smoke-filled night. Livvy looked up to see what had caused the sound.

It was the heavy wood-shake roof.

And a massive chunk gave way.

Falling.

Right toward them.

She let go of the body. Reed did the same. And they both dove to the side as the flaming wood came crashing down.

Chapter Fourteen

"What was the cause of death?" Reed asked the coroner. He had his office phone sandwiched between his ear and shoulder so he could use his hands to type the incident report on his computer.

"The obvious," Dr. McGrath answered. "Gunshot wound to the chest. The single shot hit him in the heart, and he was probably dead before the bullet even stopped moving."

Yeah. It was obvious, but Reed needed it officially confirmed. All the *i*'s had to be dotted and the *t*'s crossed. Behind him at the corner desk, Livvy was doing a report as well. He glanced at her and saw the same stark emotion in her eyes that was no doubt in his.

The adrenaline rush had long since ended for both of them. They were somewhere between the stages of shock and exhaustion, and the exhaustion was slowly but surely winning out. That was why Reed had tried to convince Livvy to go back to the inn and get some rest. He would have had better luck trying to talk a longhorn into wearing a party dress.

Still, he'd keep trying.

"The gunshot was self-inflicted?" Reed asked the coroner.

"That's my official opinion. The angle is right. So is the stippling pattern. Billy also had gunshot residue on his right hand." Dr. McGrath cursed. "How the hell did it come to this, Reed? I've known Billy for years."

"We all have." Thankfully, the fatigue allowed him to suppress the gut emotion and keep it out of his voice. "If Marcie had testified against him, Billy would have gone to jail for a long time."

That was the motive, and it was a powerful one. Everything fit. All the pieces had come together. Billy had killed Marcie, set up Shane and then tried stop Livvy and him from learning the truth.

"I need your report when it's finished," Reed told Dr. McGrath and ended the call.

Two lights were blinking on his phone, indicating he had other calls. Probably from Woody or someone else in town. Maybe even Billy's widow, Charla. The woman had called five times in the past four hours, but Reed didn't want to go another round with her trying to convince him that her husband had been set up. If Billy was innocent, then it would come through in the evidence.

"What are you reading?" Reed asked, looking over at Livvy again.

"A fax from the county sheriff's office. I asked them why they'd given Jerry the file on my mother."

"And?" Because this was something Reed wanted to know as well.

"Apparently, Jerry asked a clerk, who also happens to be his cousin, to get the file for him. Jerry thought I would jump on this lead and wouldn't focus on Jonah, his client."

Damn. Talk about a slimy move. "I hope the clerk was fired."

"He was."

That was a start, but Reed would have a long talk with Jerry about dredging up old wounds just so he could try to help out his client.

Reed ignored the blinking lights on the phone, stood and went to Livvy. Reed caught onto her arm and lifted her from the chair. She wobbled a little, and he noticed her hand was still trembling.

"It's past midnight," he reminded her. "You need some rest."

She opened her mouth, probably to argue with him, but Reed opened his, too. He started to tell her that he could carry her out of there, caveman style. But he re-thought that and simply said, "Please."

Livvy blinked. Closed her mouth. That *please* apparently took away any fight left in her, and she sagged against him as they made their way out the door.

The receptionist had gone home hours earlier, and the front office was staffed with loaner deputies, some of whom he barely knew. But Shane was there, and even though he probably needed some rest, too, Reed preferred to have his own men in the thick of things.

"We'll be back in a couple of hours," Reed told Shane. But Reed hoped he could extend that couple of hours until morning. Maybe he'd need a few more *please*s to get Livvy to shut her eyes and try to recover from yet another attempt to kill her.

"I'm waiting on a call about that glove we found in Billy's trash," Livvy said as they walked out. "And that piece of paper that dropped from Billy's pocket. It was too burned for me to read, but I'm hoping the lab will be able to tell us what it says."

"Don't worry," Reed assured her. "They'll call one of us on our cells when the tests are back." Even though it was a short walk, he helped her into his truck so he could drive her to the inn.

She wearily shook her head. "That glove is critical. My equipment bag was destroyed in the fire."

Reed didn't respond to that except with a heavy sigh that he just couldn't bite back. Fires, rattlesnakes and bullets. All of which had been used to get to Livvy. Billy had certainly been persistent.

And maybe he hadn't acted alone.

That thought had been circling around in Reed's mind since he'd seen Billy's body propped against the house. Of course, there was no proof of an accomplice, but once they'd gotten some rest he'd look into it.

Reed stopped his truck in front of the inn, and Livvy didn't protest when he helped her out and went inside. Her silence bothered him almost as much as the trembling. He grabbed the spare room key from the reception desk and led her up the stairs.

"You okay?" he asked her.

A soft burst of air left her mouth. Almost a laugh. But it wasn't from humor. "I'm fine," she lied. Her eyes met his as he unlocked her door. "You?"

"I'm fine," he lied right back.

She stopped in the doorway and stared at him. "Your friend tried to kill you tonight."

Hearing those words aloud packed a punch. "He tried to kill you, too."

"Yes, but I didn't know him the way you did. He certainly wasn't my friend." She touched his arm. Rubbed gently. "I'm worried about you, Reed."

Now, it was his turn to nearly laugh. "You're worried about me? No need. I'm worried about you."

Livvy broke the stare, turned and went into the room. But she didn't turn on the light. "No need," she repeated. "True, I'd never really had my life on the line until I came to Comanche Creek, but this baptism by fire will give me a lot of experience to deal with future cases."

That sounded, well, like something a peace officer would say. But he knew for a fact that this particular peace officer wasn't made of stone. He reached for her, but she moved away from him and waved him off.

"Not a good idea," she insisted. "If you touch me, we'll end up kissing. And then we'll have aftermath sex. It won't be real. We'll be doing it to make ourselves forget just how close we came to dying tonight."

Now, that sounded too damn logical. And she was right. If he touched her, they would kiss, and they would have sex. But Reed was afraid she was wrong about the "not being real" part. He figured Livvy was afraid of that, too.

"I'll take a nap," she continued. "Then, I'll pack." Thanks to moonlight filtering through the gauzy curtains, he could see her dodge his gaze. "Because once the lab confirms that Marcie's blood was on that glove we found in Billy's trash can, the case will be over. I'll need to head back to my office. And Comanche Creek can start returning to normal."

That did it. All this calm logic was pissing him off. So did her packing remark. Yeah, it was stupid, but Reed figured if he didn't do this, then he would regret it for the rest of his life.

He slid his hand around the back of her neck, hauled her to him and kissed her.

Reed expected her to put up at least some token resistance, but she didn't. Livvy latched on to him and returned the kiss as if this would be the one and only time it would ever happen.

Her taste slammed into him. Not the fatigue and the fear. This was all heat and silk. All woman. And the kiss quickly turned French and desperate.

She hoisted herself up, wrapping her legs around his waist, while they continued to wage war on each other's mouths. Reed stumbled, hoping they'd land on the bed, but instead his back slammed into the wall. He'd have bruises.

He didn't care.

Nothing mattered right now but taking Livvy.

She took those frantic kisses to his neck and caused him to lose his breath for a moment or two. Turnabout was fair play so he delivered some neck kisses to her as well and was rewarded with a long, feminine moan of pleasure. So Reed took his time with that particular part of her body.

Or at least that was what he tried to do.

Livvy obviously had other ideas about how fast this was all moving. Her hands were as frantic as her mouth, and she began to fight with the buttons on his shirt. She didn't even bother with the shoulder holster, and speed became even more of a necessity.

Reed tried to slow things down a bit because he wanted to add at least a little foreplay to this, but foreplay didn't stand a chance when Livvy got his shirt unbuttoned. She unhooked her legs from his waist and slid down so she could drop some tongue kisses on his chest. And his stomach.

All right, that did it.

To hell with foreplay because she was playing dirty in the best way possible. Every part of his body was on fire, and sex with Livvy was going to happen *now.*

LIVVY COULDN'T THINK. Didn't want to think. But she did want to feel, and Reed was certainly making sure that was happening. For the first time in years, every part of her felt alive.

And needed.

Reed was making sure of that as well.

Livvy had him pressed against the wall, literally, and they were both grappling at each other's shirts. Even though Livvy had his open, she still lost the particular battle when Reed threw open her shirt, shoved down her bra and took her left nipple into his mouth.

Everything went blurry and fiery hot.

She had to stop kissing him. Because she couldn't catch her breath. She could only stand there while Reed took her to the only place she wanted to go.

Well, almost.

The breast kisses sent her body flying, but soon, very soon, they weren't nearly enough. She needed more, and she knew just how to get it.

Livvy went after his belt and somehow managed to get it undone. He didn't stop those mindless kisses, making her task even harder, but she finally got the belt unlooped from his jeans, and she shoved down his zipper. She would have gotten her hand inside his boxers, too, if he hadn't pushed the two of them toward the bed. Not gently either.

But she didn't want gentleness anyway.

This was how she'd known it would be with Reed. Intense. Frantic. Hot. Memorable. So memorable that she knew he was a man she'd never forget.

In the back of her mind she thought of the broken heart that was just down the road for her. Their relationship couldn't be permanent. This would have to be it. But even one time with Reed would be worth a lifetime with anyone else.

A thought that scared her.

And got her even hotter.

Because even in the heat of the moment, Livvy knew this wasn't ordinary.

Another push from Reed, and they landed on the bed, with him on top of her. The kisses took on a new urgency. And a new location. With her shirt still wide open, he used that clever mouth on her stomach and circled her navel with his tongue.

He went lower.

And lower.

Kissing her through her jeans and making her very aware yet again of just how good this was going to be.

She felt him kick off his boots and tried to do the same. It didn't work, and Livvy cursed the difficulty of clothing removal when both of them were dressed in way too much and were way too ready for sex.

Livvy changed their positions, flipping Reed on his back so she could reach down and drag off the boots. Reed helped himself to her zipper and peeled off her jeans.

Her panties, too.

With her thighs and sex now bare, she became all too

aware that he was still wearing jeans, a barrier she didn't want between them.

Reed obviously felt the same because he turned them again until he was on top. Both grabbed his jeans, pulling and tearing at the denim. Livvy considered trying to use a little finesse but gave up when the jeans and boxers came off and she had a mostly naked Reed between her legs.

"Condom?" he ground out. "I don't have one with me."

"I'm on the pill," she answered, though she didn't try to explain she was taking them to regulate her periods. For once she praised that particular problem because without it, there would have been no birth control pills. And no sex tonight with Reed.

Livvy wasn't sure either of them would have survived that. This suddenly felt as necessary as the blood rushing through her body.

They both still had on their shoulder holsters and weapons, and the gun metal clanged against the metal when Reed grabbed on to her hair, pulled back her head and kissed her. No ordinary kiss. His tongue met hers at the exact second he entered her.

He tried to be gentle.

Livvy could tell.

But gentleness didn't stand a chance tonight. She dug her heels into the soft mattress and lifted her hips, causing him to slide hard and deep into her. She stilled just a moment. So did Reed.

And in the moon-washed room, their eyes met.

Livvy wanted the fast and furious pace to continue. She didn't want to think about the intimacy of this now. But Reed forced her to do just that. The stare lingered, piercing through her. Until she could take no more. She grabbed on to his hips and drew him into a rhythm that would satiate her body.

Too soon.

She couldn't hang on to the moment. Instead, Livvy gave in to that rhythm as well. She moved, meeting him thrust for thrust, knowing that each one was taking them closer and closer to the brink.

Livvy heard herself say something, though she hadn't intended to speak. But she did. In that moment when she could take no more of the heat, no more of those rhythmic strokes deep inside her…

She said Reed's name, repeating it with each breath she took.

And then she surrendered.

Chapter Fifteen

Reed forced his eyes open. His body was still exhausted, but humming, and already nudging him for a second round with Livvy. It wouldn't happen.

Well, not anytime soon.

She needed to sleep, and what he wanted to do with her involved the opposite of sleeping.

Reed checked the blood-red dial on the clock next to the bed. Four o'clock. Livvy and he had been asleep for nearly three hours, more than just the catnap stage. He should get up and make some calls to find out what was going on at the station.

Livvy's bare left leg was slung over him, and he eased it aside. She reached for him, groping blindly, and Reed brushed a kiss on her hand before moving it aside as well. Even though he kept everything light and soft, Livvy still woke up.

"I fell asleep," she grumbled and started to climb out of bed as well.

"And you need to keep on sleeping."

"So do you, but you're up."

He couldn't argue with that. Heck, he couldn't argue

with his body, which was begging him to climb back into bed with her. She was a sight, all right. Naked, except for her rumpled white shirt and bra that was unhooked in the front. That gave him a nice peek-a-boo view of her breasts.

And the rest of her.

Later, after he'd cleared up some things at work, he would see if he could coax her into taking a shower with him. Reed was already fantasizing about having those long athletic legs wrapped around him.

He had to do something to stave off an erection, so he pulled on his boxers and jeans. He, too, still wore his shirt, and it was a wrinkled mess. He also had a bruise on the side of his chest where his gun and holster had gouged him during sex. Livvy and he hadn't gotten around to removing their weapons until they'd finished with each other.

"I need to call the lab," she explained. She peeled off her shirt and bra, leaving herself naked.

There wasn't enough devotion to duty in the world that would make Reed pass up this opportunity. He caught her arm, pulled her to him and kissed her.

She melted against him.

She smelled like sex. Looked like sex. And that was sex melt. A hot body slide against his that let him know it wouldn't take much coaxing to get her back in bed.

Reed pulled away, looked down at her. "Give me just a minute to check in at work. *Just a minute,*" he emphasized.

Smiling, she kissed him again. "Tempting. Very tempting," Livvy added, skimming her fingers along his bare chest. "But we both need to take care of a few things. Then, before I leave, maybe we can spend some time together."

Before I leave.

Yeah. Reed had known that was coming. Still, work could wait at least another half hour, so he leaned in to convince her of that. Their mouths had barely met when the ringing sound had them jumping apart. It was his cell, and when he checked the ID screen, he knew it was a call he had to take.

"Shane," Reed answered.

But before Shane could respond, Livvy's cell phone rang as well.

"We have a problem," Shane explained. "Charla Whitley's out front, and she's got a gun pointed at her head. She says she'll kill herself if we try to come any closer. I've cleared the area, but I haven't had any luck talking her into surrendering."

Hell. Charla was obviously distraught, and with good reason, since only hours earlier she'd lost her husband. "Has she made any specific demands?" Reed wanted to know.

"She's insisted on speaking to you—and to Sergeant Hutton. I wouldn't advise that, by the way. Personally, I think Charla wants to kill both of you because she blames you for Billy's death."

Of course she did. Charla certainly wouldn't want to blame her own husband, even though the guilt might solely be on Billy's shoulders.

"I'll be there in a few minutes," Reed informed him. "I'll drive around back so Charla can't get off an easy shot at me, but if she moves, let me know."

"Will do, Reed. Right now, she's hiding in the shrubs on the west side of the building. Be careful."

Oh, he intended to do that. After he talked Livvy into staying put so she could get some more rest. However, he quickly realized that would be a losing battle because Livvy was dressing as she talked on the phone. Since he couldn't make heads nor tails of her conversation, he finished putting on his clothes as well.

"Charla's at the station," Reed explained the moment she ended her call. "She's demanding to speak to us."

Livvy blew out a long breath and shook her head. "So, we'll *speak* to her." She collected her boots from the floor. "That was the lab. The blood on the glove was a match to Marcie James. Billy's DNA was on it as well, and in the right place this time. The DNA inside the finger portions of the glove was his."

So, there it was, the proof that connected Billy to Marcie's murder. "What about the charred piece of paper that fell out of his pocket?"

Livvy sat down on the bed and pulled on her boots. "It was a suicide note. Handwritten. Billy confessed to all the murders and the attempts to kill us. The lab tech pulled up Billy's signature from his driver's license, and the handwriting seems to be a match."

Seems. Reed wanted more. After the fiasco with Shane, he wanted layers and layers of proof. "I'll send them more samples of Billy's handwriting so they can do a more thorough analysis. What about fingerprints on the paper? Did they find any?"

"Just Billy's." She hooked her bra, ending his peep show, and grabbed a fresh white shirt from the closet.

That could mean that Billy had indeed written it—

voluntarily. But maybe it meant he was coerced and the coercer had worn gloves or perhaps not even touched the paper.

But he didn't want to borrow trouble. Everything pointed to Billy, and for now, Reed would go with that.

Livvy and he strapped on their holsters, and as they hurried down the stairs, she gathered her hair back into a ponytail. They obviously woke Betty Alice because the woman threw open the door to her apartment and peered out at them.

"Is there more trouble?" she asked.

"Could be." Reed tried not to look overly alarmed about the situation with Charla. And he also tried not to look as if he'd just had sex with Livvy. It wouldn't matter, of course. The gossips would soon speculate about both, especially since his truck had been parked in front of the inn for several hours.

Betty Alice clutched the front of her pink terry-cloth robe, hugging it even tighter. "Anything I can do?"

"Just stay put. And you go ahead and lock your door."

Her eyes widened, and she gave an alarmed nod, but she shut the door, and Reed heard her double-lock it.

Livvy and he headed out, locking the front door securely behind them. They hadn't even made it down the steps when his phone rang again. From the caller ID, he could see it was Shane.

"Reed, you said you wanted to know if the situation changed," Shane said, his words rushed and laced with concern. "Well, it changed. Charla disappeared."

Reed's stomach knotted. "What do you mean she disappeared?"

"She'd been hiding in the bushes like I said, and I had one of the deputies on the top floor using night goggles to keep an eye on her. She started running, and the deputy didn't want to shoot her in the back."

Reed could understand that, especially since Charla hadn't actually threatened anyone but herself.

"I'm in pursuit of her," Shane added. "And we're both on foot."

"What direction is Charla running?" Reed asked.

Shane didn't hesitate. "She's headed your way."

WHEN REED drew his gun, Livvy did the same.

She hadn't heard all of Reed's conversation, but the last part had come through in Reed's suddenly tense expression.

What direction is Charla running?

"She's on her way here?" Livvy clarified.

"Yeah. And according to Shane, she's armed and possibly gunning for us."

Great. Here, Livvy had thought they'd dealt with the last of the attempts to kill them, but she had perhaps been wrong.

"Go after Charla," Reed instructed Shane. "But don't fire unless it's absolutely necessary. We don't know her intentions, and she could mean us no harm." Though Reed didn't sound as if he believed that.

Reed ended the call, and changed the phone's setting so that it would vibrate and not ring. He put away his phone, but he didn't hurry to his truck, probably because it was parked out in the open and not far up the street from the police station. Charla could possibly be on the very sidewalk next to the truck and ready to take aim if either Reed or Livvy stepped toward the vehicle.

"We need to take cover," Reed insisted, tipping his head to the four-foot-high limestone wall that stretched across the entire front and side yards of the inn.

Reed took the left side of the gate, and Livvy took the right. Both crouched low so they wouldn't be easy targets.

And they waited.

Because of the late hour, there were no people out and about. Thank goodness. There was little noise as well. The only sounds came from the soft hum of the streetlights and the muggy night breeze stirring the shrubs and live oak trees. What Livvy didn't hear were any footsteps, but that didn't mean Charla wasn't nearby.

The woman was apparently distraught and ready to do something stupid to avenge her husband's suicide. That meant Reed and she had to be prepared for anything, and that included defending themselves if Charla couldn't be stopped some other way. Livvy didn't want it to come down to that. There had already been enough deaths and shootings in Comanche Creek without adding a recent widow to the list.

Livvy heard a soft creaking noise and lifted her head a fraction so she could try to determine where the sound had originated.

"Behind us," Reed whispered. He turned in the direction of the inn. "Keep watch on the front."

Livvy did, and she tried to keep her breathing quiet enough so it wouldn't give away their positions. It would be safer for everyone if they could get the jump on Charla and disarm her before she had a chance to use her gun.

There was another sound. Maybe the leaves rustling in the wind. But Livvy got the sickening feeling in the pit of her stomach that it was much more than that.

Maybe even footsteps.

The sound was definitely coming from behind them, where there was no fence, only the lush gardens that Betty Alice kept groomed to perfection. Did that mean Charla had changed course so she could ambush them? If so, maybe the woman wasn't quite as distraught as everyone thought she was.

She could possibly even be her husband's accomplice.

That wasn't a crazy theory, since Billy had no doubt profited from the sale of the land that Jonah had ended up buying. Maybe Charla hadn't gotten personally involved and had no idea it would lead to her husband's death.

"My phone," Reed whispered, reaching into his pocket. It'd apparently vibrated to indicate he had a call.

Reed glanced down at the back-lit caller ID screen and put the phone to his mouth. "Shane?" His voice was barely audible, and she was too far away to make out a single word of what Shane was saying.

She continued to wait. The seconds ticked off in Livvy's head, and she held her breath for what seemed to be an eternity. She cursed the fatigue and the fog in her head. She needed to think clearly, but the lack of sleep and the adrenaline were catching up with her.

Reed finally eased the phone shut and slid it back into his pocket. His expression said it all—he was not a happy man. "Charla got into her car and drove off. Kirby and another deputy are in pursuit. Shane's staying at the station in case she heads back there."

"Shane's alone?" she asked.

Reed nodded.

Livvy glanced up both ends of the street. There were no signs of an approaching vehicle. Well, no headlights anyway, but if the car was dark-colored, Charla might have turned off her lights so she could get close to them without being detected.

"You think she'll come this way?" Livvy asked.

"No." But then he lifted his shoulder. "Not unless she doubles back."

Which she could do. *Easily.* After all, Main Street wasn't the only way to get to the inn. She could park on one of the back streets and make her way through the inn's garden.

Of course, that was only one of many places Charla could end up. She might have other people she wanted to confront—including Jonah Becker.

"You should get to the station so Shane will have some backup," Livvy reminded him. "But I'm concerned about leaving Betty Alice here alone. If Charla does double back, she might come here and try to get in."

His gaze met hers, and there was plenty enough light for her to see the argument he was having with himself. Livvy decided to go on the offensive.

"I'm not a civilian, Reed. I'm trained to do exactly this sort of thing."

Reed scowled. "If I leave, then you don't have backup."

"True. But I can go inside. Stand guard. And I can call you if something goes wrong."

He continued to stare and scowl at her. A dozen things passed between them. An argument. Some emotion. Also the reminder that they weren't just partners on a case. Sex had changed things.

But it couldn't stay that way.

Both of them were married to their badges, and they couldn't let sex—even the best sex ever—get in the way of what had to be done.

Livvy tried to give him one last reassuring glance before she checked the street and surrounding area.

No sign of Charla.

"Go to the station," she insisted.

"No." He matched her insistent tone. "We both go, and we'll take Betty Alice with us."

Livvy huffed to show her disapproval at the veto of her plan, but she had to admit it was, well, reasonable. Or at least it would be if they could get Betty Alice safely out. Livvy didn't like the idea of a civilian being brought out into the open when a shooter might be in the area.

"The inn doesn't have a garage," she commented, looking at the house. "Maybe you should pull the truck to the back, and we can get Betty Alice out through the kitchen."

Reed nodded. "Call her and let her know the plan. Then we'll get in the truck together. I don't want to leave you out here waiting."

Livvy took out her phone, and for a moment she thought the sound she heard was from her hand brushing against the pocket of her jeans.

It wasn't.

The sound was footsteps. Frantic ones. And they had definitely come from behind.

Both Reed and she spun in that direction. They had their guns aimed and ready. But neither of them fired.

Livvy tried to pick through the murky shadows in the shrub-dotted yard to see who or what was out there. She didn't see anyone, but that didn't mean they weren't there.

She tightened her grip on her pistol. Waited. And prayed.

The next sound wasn't a footstep. More like a rustling. And she was able to determine that it had come from a cluster of mountain laurels on the west side of the yard.

She aimed her gun in that direction.

Just as the shot blasted through the silence.

Livvy didn't even have time to react. But she certainly felt it.

The bullet slammed right into her.

Chapter Sixteen

Everything happened fast, but to Reed, it felt as if he were suddenly moving in slow motion.

He saw the bullet slam into Livvy's left shoulder. He saw the shock on her face.

The blood on her shirt.

Cursing, he scrambled to her and pulled her down onto the ground so she wouldn't be hit again. It wasn't a moment too soon because another shot came flying their way.

"Livvy?" he managed to say, though he couldn't ask how badly she was hurt. That was because his breath and his heart were jammed in his throat.

She had to be okay.

"I'm fine," she ground out.

But it was another lie. The blood was already spreading across her sleeve, and she dropped her gun.

Though the shots continued to come at them, Reed didn't return fire. He ripped off the sleeve of his shirt and used it to apply pressure to the wound.

The bullet had gone into the fleshy part of her

shoulder. Or at least that was what he hoped. Still, that was only a few inches from her heart.

He'd come damn close to losing her.

The rage raced through him, and he took Livvy's hand, placing it against her wound so he could return fire and stop the shooter from moving any closer. He hoped he could blast this SOB for what he'd done.

Or rather what *she* had done.

Charla.

She must have doubled back after all.

Reed sent a couple of shots the shooter's way and took out his phone. He didn't bother with dispatch. He called Shane.

"I need an ambulance. Livvy's been shot. Approach the inn with caution because we're under attack." That was all he had time to say because he didn't want to lose focus on either Livvy or the gunman.

"I'm okay," Livvy insisted. Wincing, she picked up her gun, and holding it precariously, she also tried to keep some pressure on her bleeding shoulder.

"You're not okay," Reed countered. He maneuvered himself in front of her with his back to her so he could keep an eye on the shooter. "But you will be. Shane will be here soon to provide backup, and he's getting an ambulance out here."

She shook her head. "It won't be safe for the medics. We need to take care of this before they get here."

Livvy was right. It was standard procedure to secure the scene before bringing in medical personnel, but Reed wasn't sure he could take the risk of Livvy bleeding to death. Somehow, he had to get her to the hospital, even if he had to drive her there himself.

He glanced back at the truck.

It was a good twenty feet away, and they'd be right in the line of fire if they stood. That meant Reed had to draw this moron out because he couldn't waste any more time with the attack.

The shots were all coming from the side of the house near some shrubs. It was a dark murky space, most likely why the shooter had chosen it. But it wasn't the only shadowy place. He, too, could use the shrubs and get closer so he could launch his own assault.

Reed looked over his shoulder at Livvy. "Can you shoot if necessary?"

She winced again and forced out a rough breath. But she nodded. "I can shoot."

"Then I'm going out there." He wanted to take a moment to tell her to be safe. To hang in there. Hell, he even wanted to wait until Shane had arrived, but all of that would eat up precious seconds.

Time they didn't have.

Crouched down, Reed inched forward and kept his gun ready in case the shooter came running out of those shrubs and across the lawn. But there was no movement. And the only sound was from the shots that were coming about ten seconds apart.

He went even closer to the shooter, but then stopped when he heard the footsteps. They weren't coming from in front of him, but rather from behind.

"Shane?" Reed said softly.

No answer.

And the shots stopped.

Hell. He turned so he could cover both sides in case the shooter was making his move to get closer. As Livvy leaned against the wall for support, she lifted her gun and aimed it as well.

They waited there, eating up precious moments while Livvy continued to lose blood.

"Shane?" Reed tried again.

"No," someone answered.

Definitely not Shane. It was a woman's voice, and a quick glance at Livvy let him know that she was as stunned as he was.

"It's me, Charla," the woman said.

Since her voice was coming from the area by the gate, an area that was much too close to Livvy, Reed hurried back in that direction.

Just as Charla dove through the gate opening.

Reed caught just a glimpse of her gun, and his gut clenched. No! He couldn't let Charla shoot Livvy again.

This time, the bullet might be fatal.

Charla landed chest-first on the ground, her gun trapped beneath her. Livvy moved, adjusting her position so she could aim her gun at the woman.

Reed did more than that. He launched himself toward Charla and threw his body on hers so she couldn't be able to maneuver her weapon out into the open.

There wasn't time to negotiate Charla's surrender, so Reed grabbed her right wrist and wrenched the gun from her hand. He tossed it toward Livvy and then shoved his forearm against the back of Charla's neck to keep her pinned to the ground.

"Call Shane," Reed instructed Livvy. "Tell him to get that ambulance here now."

With her breath racing and her chest pumping for breath, Livvy took out her phone. Beneath him, Charla didn't struggle, but she did lift her head and look around. Her eyes were wild, and Reed could feel her pulse racing out of control.

"Who was shooting at you?" Charla asked.

The question caused both Livvy and Reed to freeze.

"You," Reed reminded her.

Charla frantically shook her head. "No. It wasn't me. I didn't fire my gun. I heard the shots and took cover on the other side of the fence."

Reed was about to call her a liar, but he didn't manage to get the word out of his mouth. That was because the next sound turned his blood to ice.

Someone fired another bullet at them.

LIVVY DROPPED back to the ground.

Her wounded shoulder smashed against the limestone fence, and the pain shot through her. She gasped, causing Reed's gaze to whip in her direction.

"I'm okay," she lied again.

The pain was excruciating, and the front of her shirt was wet with her own blood. She needed a doctor, but a doctor wasn't going to do any of them any good if the shooter managed to continue.

And obviously, the shooter wasn't Charla.

Mercy, what was going on?

Livvy had been so sure those shots had come from the grieving widow, but obviously she'd been wrong. Someone else was out there, and this person wanted them dead.

But who?

There was another shot. Another. Then another. Each of the thick blasts slammed through the air and landed

God knew where. Livvy prayed that none of them were landing inside the inn, and while she was at it, she also prayed that Betty Alice would stay put and not come racing out in fear.

Livvy waited. Listening. But the shots didn't continue. That was both good and bad. She certainly didn't want Reed to be wounded, or worse, but the lack of shots could mean the gunman was on the move.

Maybe coming straight toward them.

She heard the sirens from the ambulance and saw the red lights knifing through the darkness. But the lights didn't come closer, and the sirens stopped, probably because Shane had told them to stay back. Livvy hadn't managed to call him as Reed had ordered. And that was a good thing. If she had, if she'd told them that Reed had the shooter subdued, the medics would have driven straight into what could be a death trap.

Reed jerked his phone from his pocket, and since the screen was already lit, it meant he had a call.

"Shane," Reed answered. "Where are you?"

Because Reed had his hands full with the call, keeping watch and with Charla, Livvy hoisted herself back up to a sitting position so she could return fire if necessary. Maybe, just maybe, her body would cooperate. The pain was making it hard to focus, and Livvy was afraid she wouldn't be able to hear anything over her heartbeat pounding in her ears.

"We don't know who the gunman is," Reed told Shane. "But it's not Charla. She's with us." He paused, apparently listening to Shane. "Okay. But Livvy and Charla are staying put. Call Livvy if there's a change in plans."

With that, Reed shut his phone and shoved it back

into his pocket. "Shane's going to try to sneak up on the gunman," he whispered. "And I need to help him."

Livvy understood. Reed couldn't help if he had to hang on to Charla. Though it took several deep breaths and a lot of willpower to force herself to move, Livvy reached out with her left hand and began to pull Charla in her direction. Reed moved to the side, and together they maneuvered the woman in place just to the side of Livvy.

Charla didn't resist.

She went willingly and pressed her body against the fence. She also covered her face with her hands. Livvy didn't think the woman was faking her fear, so that probably meant Charla had no idea who their attacker was.

"I'm going straight ahead," Reed mouthed. But he didn't move. He paused just a moment to meet her gaze, and then he started to crawl forward again.

"Don't get hurt," Livvy mumbled under her breath, but she was sure he didn't hear her.

She instantly regretted that she hadn't said more, something with more emotion and volume. But that would have been a stupid thing to do. Reed didn't need emotion from her now. He needed her to keep Charla subdued and safe, and for that to happen, she had to stay alert and conscious.

The next shot put her right back on high alert. The bullet slammed into the limestone just inches from Charla's head. Charla yelped and dropped on her stomach to the ground, and Livvy sank lower. She couldn't go belly-down as Charla had done, she needed to be able to help Reed, but she did slide slightly lower.

Another bullet.

This one hit just inches from the last one. God, she hoped the shooter hadn't managed to pinpoint them somehow. But there was some good in this because the shots didn't seem to be aimed at Reed.

She heard Reed move forward, making his way across the lawn. Livvy couldn't see him, but she knew he would use the shrubs for cover. Maybe that would be enough, but bullets could easily go through plants and leaves. She choked back the rest of that realization because the physical pain was one thing, but she couldn't bear the thought of Reed being hurt.

Beside her, Charla began to sob. Livvy was about to try to stop her when her phone rang. Unlike Reed, she hadn't put hers on vibrate, so the ringing sound was loud.

There was a shot fired.

Then another.

The third one bashed into the limestone and sent a spray of stone chips flying through the air. Livvy tried to shield her eyes, and she snatched up her phone so it wouldn't ring again.

"It's me, Shane," the caller said.

Livvy released the breath she'd been holding. It wasn't Reed calling to tell her that he'd taken one of those bullets.

"Where's Reed?"

"I'm not sure. Somewhere between the fence and the west side of the inn." She tried to pick through the darkness and shadows, but she couldn't see him either. "Where are you?"

"The back porch of the inn. I'm going to try to sneak up the stairs to the upper porch."

It was a good idea. That way, he might be able to spot the shooter. If the shooter didn't spot Shane first, that was. The outside stairs weren't exactly concealed, and the shooter might have an unobstructed view of both the stairs and the upper porch.

"Be careful," Livvy warned. "But hurry. Whoever's doing this isn't giving up."

She got instant proof of that. The shooter fired again, and this time the bullet didn't go into the fence. It went into the wooden gate just on the other side of Charla. The woman screamed, covered her head with her hands and tried to scramble behind Livvy.

"Were you hit again?" Shane immediately asked.

"No." Livvy pressed the phone between her right shoulder and ear so she could focus on keeping aim. No easy feat. The pain was worse now, and it seemed to be throbbing through every inch of her body.

"Just hang in there," Shane told her. "We'll get the medics in ASAP."

He'd obviously heard the pain come through in her voice. Livvy hoped the shooter didn't sense that as well because she was in no shape to win a gunfight.

"I've got to hang up now," Shane continued. "I'm at the stairs, and— Wait…"

That *wait* got Livvy's complete attention. "What's wrong?"

"I see the shooter. He's wearing dark clothes, and he's behind the oak tree."

Not the mountain laurels as Reed had thought. She quickly tried to remember the landscape, and if her memory was right, Reed could soon be crawling right past the gunman.

Or right at him.

Shane cursed, and the call ended.

Livvy mumbled some profanity as well. She considered phoning Reed but figured it was too late for that.

"Reed?" she shouted. "Watch out!"

But her warning was drowned out by the gunfire that blasted through the air. Not from the direction where the shooter had originally been.

The shots came from directly in front of them.

Chapter Seventeen

Reed heard Livvy's warning, but it was too late for him to do anything but duck his head and hope the bullets missed him.

And her.

God knew how much pain Livvy was in right now, and she certainly wasn't in any shape to be in the middle of this mess.

"Stay down!" Reed called out to Livvy, Charla and Shane.

He hoped they all listened and had the capability to keep out of the line of fire. Shane certainly wasn't in the best of positions. Or at least he hadn't been when Reed had last spotted his deputy at the base of the stairs. Then Shane had disappeared, and Reed hoped like hell that he'd taken cover.

Since there was no safe way for him to go forward and because he was worried about Livvy, Reed turned and began to make his way back to her. It was obvious the gunman was on the move, and Reed didn't want him to manage to sneak up on Livvy.

Moving as fast as he could while trying to keep his

ear attuned to the directions of the shots, Reed maneuvered his way through the damp grass and the shrubs. He spotted Livvy. She was crouched over Charla, protecting her, but Reed knew Livvy needed someone to protect her.

God, there was even more blood on her shirt.

He scrambled to her, keeping low because of the barrage of bullets, and he clamped his hand over her wound again. It wasn't gushing blood, but even a trickle could cause her to bleed out.

"We can't wait for the ambulance," he whispered. "I need to get you out of here."

She didn't argue. Well, not verbally anyway. He saw the argument in the depths of her eyes, but he also saw that the blood loss had weakened her.

"I'm going to stay in front of you," he instructed Livvy. "Do you think you can crawl through the gate and onto the sidewalk?"

"Yes." Now, she shook her head. "But I won't leave you here to fend for yourself."

He nearly laughed. *Nearly.* So, there was some fight left in her after all. "I have Shane for backup. I'll cover you while you get to the sidewalk. Get as far away from the inn as you can, and I'll have the medics meet you."

Charla moved when Livvy did, but Reed latched on to the woman. "You're staying here." Though he doubted Charla was truly involved in the shooting, he didn't want Livvy to have to worry about watching her back.

Livvy had barely made it to the gate when Reed heard the sound. Not more gunfire, but movement. It wasn't just footsteps either. There seemed to be some kind of altercation going on, and whatever it was, it was happening in front of them.

Shane.

Hell, his deputy had likely come face-to-face with the gunman.

Reed motioned for Livvy to keep moving, but she didn't. She stopped and aimed her gun in the direction of those sounds. Someone cursed. It was definitely Shane, and then there was a loud thump. Reed had been around enough fights to know that someone had just connected with a punch.

The silence returned.

But it didn't last.

It was mere seconds before the footsteps started. This wasn't a quiet skulking motion. Someone was running straight toward them.

Reed couldn't call out Shane's name because it would give away Livvy's and his positions. Besides, whoever this was, it wasn't Shane. His deputy was well-trained and would have identified himself to avoid being shot.

The gunman darted out from one of the eight-foot-high mountain laurels.

Reed fired.

And missed.

But he'd gotten a glimpse of the person. Shane was right about the dark clothes, and it was definitely a man.

Reed got a sickening feeling. He hoped it wasn't Woody out there.

The shots started again, and the man rushed out, coming closer. Each shot and each movement was wasting time, and Reed was fed up. He needed to get Livvy out of there.

He motioned for Livvy to stay down. Whether she would or not was anyone's guess. Reed picked up a chunk of the limestone that'd broken off in the attack, and tossed it to the center of the yard. When the stone landed on the ground, the gunman left cover.

Reed fired again.

This time, he didn't miss.

The shooter howled in pain and clamped his hands onto his left thigh.

"Fire a couple of shots into the ground but in that direction and then get to the medics," he told Livvy, pointing to the area on the west side of the inn but still far enough away from where he would be heading. He needed a diversion in case their attacker could still manage to shoot.

Reed hurried, racing toward the gunman who'd done his level best to kill them. And this wasn't over. He had no idea just how badly Livvy, and maybe even Shane, were hurt. There had to be a good reason his deputy wasn't responding.

When he was closer, Reed saw that the shooter was wearing a black baseball cap that was tilted down to cover the upper portion of his face. Reed didn't stop or take the time to figure out who this was; he dove at the guy.

The shooter lifted his gun.

Aimed.

But he didn't get off another shot before Reed plowed right into him.

Both of them went to the ground, hard, and the guy's gun rammed into Reed's rib cage. It nearly knocked the breath right out of him, but Reed fought to pull air into his lungs while he fought to hang on to his gun.

But he wasn't successful.

The man swiped at Reed's arm, and it was just enough to send his weapon flying.

Still, Reed wasn't about to give up. He used every bit of his anger and adrenaline so he could slam his fist into the man's face.

It worked.

The guy's head flopped back. He wasn't unconscious, but the movement caused his baseball cap to fall off. And Reed got a close look at the gunman's face.

He cursed.

Because it was a face he knew all too well.

The shock stunned Reed for a moment. Just a moment. But that was apparently all the time the man needed to get his weapon back into place.

The gun slammed hard against the side of Reed's head.

LIVVY COULD no longer feel the pain. That was good. Because one way or another she was going to make her way to Reed, and dealing with the pain was one less obstacle that could get in her way.

Charla was still sobbing and cowering against the fence. It was a risk to leave her there alone, but it was an even bigger risk to let Reed take on the gunman without backup. Yes, Shane was out there somewhere, but he didn't seem to be responding. She hoped he hadn't been shot, or killed.

Livvy forced herself to stand, and since there were no more bullets flying, she didn't exactly crouch. Her goal was to make it to Reed as quickly as possible.

Still, that wasn't nearly fast enough.

She felt as if she were walking through sludge, and

it didn't help that she had to keep her shooting hand clamped to her shoulder. That meant her gun was out of position if she had to fire, but she would deal with that if and when it came down to it. She couldn't let the blood flow go unchecked, or else this rescue mission would fail, and she would be in just as much serious trouble as Reed and Shane.

She trudged through the grass and shrubs, and she heard the sounds of a struggle.

Reed and the gunman, no doubt.

At least they weren't shooting at each other, and even though she dreaded the idea of Reed having to fist-fight his way out of a situation, he'd apparently cornered the shooter, and maybe that meant this was on its way to being over.

Just ahead of her, Livvy heard a different sound. Much softer and closer than the battle going on at the other side of the yard. This was a moan, and it sounded as if someone was in pain. The person was lying on the ground just ahead of her. She unclamped her arm so she could aim and moved closer.

It was Shane.

He moaned again and touched his head. "Someone knocked me out," he whispered.

Livvy didn't take the time to examine him further. The deputy was alive and could fend for himself for a little while so she could get to Reed.

She silently cursed. The sex had indeed changed everything. Or maybe the sex was just the icing on this particular cake. Livvy had to admit that the reason the sex had happened in the first place was because she'd fallen hard and fast for the hot cowboy cop.

Worse, she was in love with him.

She hadn't realized that until she'd seen him rush away after the gunman. And he'd done that to save her. That's the kind of man he was. A man worth loving. Too bad that wouldn't solve all their problems. Still, that was a matter for a different time and place. Right now, she needed to focus all her energy on helping Reed.

Oh, and she needed to stay conscious.

She didn't think she'd lost too much blood, but the shock was starting to take over. Soon, very soon, she wouldn't be much help to Reed.

"I'll be back," she whispered to Shane and stepped around him.

Livvy didn't have to walk far before she saw Reed and the other man. They were fighting, and in the darkness she couldn't tell where Reed's body began and the other man's ended. She certainly couldn't risk firing a shot because she might hit Reed.

The man bashed his forearm into Reed's throat, and Reed staggered back. She saw the blood on his face. And on the front of his shirt.

Her heart dropped.

Livvy blinked back the dizziness and raced to get closer. They were there, right in front of her, less than a yard away, but she still didn't have a clean shot, and she didn't trust her aim anyway. The shooter would have to be out in the open before she could fire, and it didn't help that the man still had a weapon in his hand.

Reed's fist connected with the man's jaw, and that put a little distance between the two. Not enough for her to fire. But enough for her to catch a glimpse of the man's face.

It was Ben Tolbert.

God, had Ben knocked out his own son? And why was he doing this? Why was he trying to kill them?

"Stay back!" Reed shouted to her.

She didn't listen. Couldn't. Ben was armed and Reed wasn't. Plus, there was all that blood on Reed's shirt.

The milky-white moon cast an eerie light on Ben, and she saw him sneer at her. And lift his gun.

Ben aimed it right at her.

Her body didn't react as quickly as her mind did. Livvy recognized the danger. She realized she was about to be shot again, but she couldn't seem to get out of the way. Nor could she shoot. That was because her hand had gone numb. So had her legs, and she felt herself start to fall.

Reed shouted something. Something she couldn't understand. And she heard the shot the moment she hit the ground. The blast was thick and loud, and it echoed through her head.

"Reed," she managed to say. She prayed the bullet hadn't slammed into him.

Forcing herself to remain conscious, she turned her head and saw Reed lunge at Ben. This time, there was no real battle. A feral sound tore from Reed's throat, and he slammed his weight into Ben. In the same motion, Reed ripped the gun from Ben's hand. Both of them landed on the grass, not far from her. And she saw Reed put the gun to Ben's head.

"Move and you die," Reed warned. Every muscle in his face had corded and was strained with raw emotion.

Ben obviously believed him because he dropped his hands in surrender.

It was over. They were safe. Now, they just needed the medics.

Livvy tried to get up so she could go find them, but she only managed to lift her head a fraction before the darkness took over and closed in around her.

Chapter Eighteen

Reed paced, because he couldn't figure out what else to do with the powder keg of energy and emotion that was boiling inside him. Waiting had never been his strong suit, and it especially wasn't when he was waiting for the latest about Livvy's condition.

He heard the footsteps in the hall that led to the E.R. waiting room and whirled in that direction. It wasn't the doctor. It was Kirby, his deputy.

"Here are the things you asked me to get," Kirby said, handing Reed the plastic grocery bag. "I don't guess they've told you anything yet?"

"No. One of the nurses came out about ten minutes ago and said I'd know something soon." But *soon* needed to be *now* when it came to Livvy. "How's Shane?"

"He's got another bump on his head, but other than that, he's fine. The doc will be releasing him soon."

Good. That was one less thing to worry about, even though this wouldn't be the end of Shane's worries. After all, his father had just tried to murder Livvy and Reed. Ben Tolbert would likely to go to jail for the rest of his life.

"I called the station on the way over here, and Ben's talking, by the way," Kirby continued. "Jerry's trying to make him hush, but Ben confessed to setting the cabin on fire and trying to scare Livvy into leaving town. He didn't want any evidence that could link Shane to Marcie's murder."

Reed felt every muscle in his body tighten. He wanted to pulverize Ben for what he'd done. "But Livvy's the one who cleared Shane's name."

Kirby shrugged. "Ben evidently thought Livvy wasn't done with Shane. He figured she'd keep looking for anything and everything to put Shane back in jail."

Great. Because of Ben's warped loyalty to his son, Livvy might have to pay a huge price.

"What about Charla?" Reed asked.

"The medics took her to Austin, to the psych ward. After they've evaluated her, they'll give you a call."

Kirby had barely finished his sentence, when Reed heard more footsteps. This time, it was Dr. Eric Callahan, the man who'd forced Reed out of the E.R. so he could get to work on Livvy's gunshot wound.

"How is she?" Reed demanded, holding his breath.

"She lost quite a bit of blood so we gave her a transfusion. She's B-negative, and thanks to you, we have a small stockpile."

"You gave her Reed's blood?" Kirby asked.

Dr. Callahan nodded, but Reed interrupted any verbal response he might have given Kirby. Yes, Reed was a regular blood donor, and he was damn thankful the supply had been there for Livvy, but a transfusion was the last thing he wanted to discuss right now.

"How's Livvy?" Reed snapped.

"She's okay. The bullet went through and doesn't appear to have damaged anything permanently—"

"I want to see her." Reed didn't wait for permission. He pushed his way past the doctor and went to the room where they'd taken Livvy nearly an hour earlier.

Reed stormed into the room but came to a dead stop. There Livvy was, lying on the bed. Awake. Her shoulder sporting a fresh bandage. Heck, she even gave him a thin smile, but she looked pale and weak. That smile, however, faded in a flash when Livvy's gaze dropped to the front of his shirt.

Reed glanced down at what had snagged her attention and immediately shook his head. "It's not mine." The blood on the front of his shirt had gotten there during his fight with Ben.

Livvy gave a sigh of relief and eased her head back onto the pillow.

"You shouldn't be in here," the nurse on the other side of the room insisted.

"I'm not leaving," Reed insisted right back. "Not until I find out how you really are," he said to Livvy.

"I'll speak to the doctor about that," the nurse warned and headed out of the room.

Livvy motioned for him to come closer. "I'm fine, *really*. The doctor gave me some good pain meds so I'm not feeling much." Her eyes met his. "Well, not much pain anyway. Please tell me Ben Tolbert is behind bars."

Reed walked closer, the plastic grocery bag swishing against the leg of his jeans. "He is. Or soon will be. I had Ben sent to the county jail. He's receiving medical treatment for the gunshot wound to his leg, but after that, he'll be going to the prison hospital."

"Good." And a moment later she repeated it.

Livvy might have been medicated, but the painkillers didn't remove the emotion from her voice or face. She'd been through hell tonight, and Reed had taken that trip right along with her.

He sat down on the right side of the bed so he wouldn't accidentally bump into her injury and, because he thought they both could use it, he leaned over and kissed Livvy. Reed intended to keep it short and sweet. Just a peck of reassurance. But Livvy slid her hand around the back of his neck and drew him closer. Even after she broke the kiss, she held him there with his forehead pressed against hers.

"I thought I'd lost you," she whispered, taking the words right out of his mouth.

Reed settled for a "Yeah," but it wasn't a casual response. His voice had as much emotion as hers, and he eased back just a little so he could meet her eye to eye. "I'm sorry I let this happen to you."

She pushed her fingers over his lips. "You didn't 'let' this happen. You did everything to save me."

He glanced down at the bandage and hated the thought that she was alive in part because they'd gotten lucky. Reed didn't want luck playing into this.

"You can't stay," someone said from the doorway. It was the doctor.

"Give me five minutes," Reed bargained. He didn't pull away from Livvy, and he didn't look back at the doctor.

"Five minutes," he finally said, and Reed heard the doctor walking away.

"Not much time," Livvy volunteered.

"Don't worry. I'll be back after you've gotten some rest." But first, he had something important to do.

He took out the candy bars from the bag and put them on the stand next to her bed.

Her face lit up. "You brought me Snickers?" She smiled and kissed him again. "You know, I could love a man who brings me chocolate."

The realization of what she'd said caused her smile to freeze, and she got that deer-caught-in-the-headlights look.

"Don't take it back," Reed blurted out.

She blinked. "Wh-what?"

"Don't take that *love a man* part back, because that's what I want you to do."

"You want me to love you?" She sounded as if he'd just requested that she hand him the moon.

And in a way, he had.

"Yeah. I do," he assured her.

But Reed lifted his hand in a wait-a-second gesture so he could lay the groundwork for this. He took out a map from the bag and fanned it open. It took him a moment to find what he was looking for.

"This is Comanche Creek," he said, pointing to the spot. "And this is Austin." He pointed to the space in between. "I want to find a house or build one halfway between. That'd give us both a thirty-minute commute to work."

And because he wanted her to think about that for

several moments, and because he didn't want her to say no, he kissed her. He didn't keep it tame, either. But then, neither did Livvy. She might have been in the E.R., but it was crystal-clear that kissing was still on the agenda.

She pulled back, ran her tongue over his bottom lip and smiled. "You want us to live together. I'd like that."

"Like?" he questioned.

Her forehead bunched up. "All right, I'd *love* to do that. You really have love on the brain tonight." She winced. "Sorry, that didn't come out right. Blame it on the pain meds."

That had him hesitating. "How clearly are you thinking?"

"Why?" she asked.

"Because I'm about to tell you that I'm in love with you, and I want to make sure you understand."

Her mouth dropped open. "You're in love with me?"

"Yeah." And Reed held his breath again. He watched her face, staring at her and trying to interpret every little muscle flicker. Every blink. Every tremble of her mouth.

"You don't love me?" he finally said.

The breath swooshed out of her and she grabbed him again and planted a very hard kiss on his mouth. "I love you. I'm in love with you. And I want to live with you in a house with a thirty-minute commute."

She smiled. It was warm and gooey, and in all his life, Reed had never been happier to see warm and gooey.

"Good," he let her know. Another kiss. Before he moved on to the next part.

"Your five minutes are up," he heard the doctor say from the doorway.

"Then give me six," Reed snarled. He tried not to snarl though when he looked down at Livvy.

"Whatever you've got to say to her, it can wait," the doctor insisted.

"No. It can't." He looked into Livvy's eyes. "I don't want to just live with you."

She shook her head. "But you said—"

"I want to marry you, and then I want us to live together."

"You're proposing?" the doctor grumbled, and Reed heard the man walk away.

"Yes, I'm proposing," Reed verified to Livvy. "And now, I'm waiting for an answer."

An answer she didn't readily give. But she did make a show of tapping her chin as if in deep thought. "Let me see. I have a really hot sheriff that I love with all my heart. He buys me chocolate and jumps out in front of snakes and bullets for me. He's also great in bed. And he wants to marry me."

Reed smiled. "Does that mean you're saying yes?"

She pulled him closer. "Yes. With one condition."

Reed could have sworn his heart stopped. He didn't want conditions. He wanted Livvy, and he wanted all of her. "What condition?" he managed to asked.

There were tears in her eyes now, but she was also still smiling.

Reed thought those might be good signs. He was sure the lusty kiss she gave him was a good sign, too.

"The condition is—this has to be forever," Livvy whispered.

Well, that was a given. "It took me thirty-two years to find you, and I have no intentions of ever letting go."

And to prove that, Reed pulled Livvy closer and kissed her.

* * * * *

THE SILVER STAR OF TEXAS:
COMANCHE CREEK
concludes next month with Rita Herron's
RAWHIDE RANGER.
Look for it wherever
Harlequin Intrigue books are sold!

*Rancher Ramsey Westmoreland's
temporary cook is way too attractive for his liking.
Little does he know Chloe Burton came to his
ranch with another agenda entirely....*

That man across the street had to be, without a doubt, the most handsome man she'd ever seen.

Chloe Burton's pulse beat rhythmically as he stopped to talk to another man in front of a feed store. He was tall, dark and every inch of sexy—from his Stetson to the well-worn leather boots on his feet. And from the way his jeans and Western shirt fit his broad muscular shoulders, it was quite obvious he had everything it took to separate the men from the boys. The combination was enough to corrupt any woman's mind and had her weakening even from a distance. Her body felt flushed. It was hot. Unsettled.

Over the past year the only male who had gotten her time and attention had been the e-mail. That was simply pathetic, especially since now she was practically drooling simply at the sight of a man. Even his stance— both hands in his jeans pockets, legs braced apart, was a pose she would carry to her dreams.

And he was smiling, evidently enjoying the conversation being exchanged. He had dimples, incredibly sexy dimples in not one but both cheeks.

"What are you staring at, Clo?"

Chloe nearly jumped. She'd forgotten she had a lunch date. She glanced over the table at her best friend from college, Lucia Conyers.

"Take a look at that man across the street in the blue shirt, Lucia. Will he not be perfect for Denver's first issue of *Simply Irresistible* or what?" Chloe asked with so much excitement she almost couldn't stand it.

She was the owner of *Simply Irresistible,* a magazine for today's up-and-coming woman. Their once-a-year Irresistible Man cover, which highlighted a man the magazine felt deserved the honor, had increased sales enough for Chloe to open a Denver office.

When Lucia didn't say anything but kept staring, Chloe's smile widened. "Well?"

Lucia glanced across the booth at her. "Since you asked, I'll tell you what I see. One of the Westmorelands—Ramsey Westmoreland. And, yes, he'd be perfect for the cover, but he won't do it."

Chloe raised a brow. "He'd get paid for his services, of course."

Lucia laughed and shook her head. "Getting paid won't be the issue, Clo—Ramsey is one of the wealthiest sheep ranchers in this part of Colorado. But everyone knows what a private person he is. Trust me—he won't do it."

Chloe couldn't help but smile. The man was the epitome of what she was looking for in a magazine cover and she was determined that whatever it took, he would be it.

"Umm, I don't like that look on your face, Chloe. I've seen it before and know exactly what it means."

She watched as Ramsey Westmoreland entered the store with a swagger that made her almost breathless. She *would* be seeing him again.

Look for Silhouette Desire's
HOT WESTMORELAND NIGHTS
by Brenda Jackson,
available March wherever books are sold.

THE WESTMORELANDS

NEW YORK TIMES
bestselling author

BRENDA JACKSON

HOT WESTMORELAND NIGHTS

Ramsey Westmoreland knew better than to lust
after the hired help. But Chloe, the new cook,
was just so delectable. Though their affair was
growing steamier, Chloe's motives became
suspicious. And when he learned Chloe was
carrying his child this Westmoreland Rancher
had to choose between pride or duty.

Available March 2010 wherever books are sold.

Always Powerful, Passionate and Provocative.

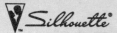

Two families torn apart by secrets and desire
are about to be reunited in

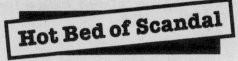

a sexy new duet by

Kelly Hunter

EXPOSED: MISBEHAVING WITH THE MAGNATE

#2905 Available March 2010

Gabriella Alexander returns to the French vineyard she
was banished from after being caught in flagrante with the
owner's son Lucien Duvalier—only to finish what they started!

REVEALED: A PRINCE AND A PREGNANCY

#2913 Available April 2010

Simone Duvalier wants Rafael Alexander and always has, but
they both get more than they bargained for when a night of
passion and a royal revelation rock their world!

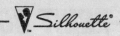

SPECIAL EDITION

FROM *USA TODAY* BESTSELLING AUTHOR

CHRISTINE RIMMER

A BRIDE FOR JERICHO BRAVO

Marnie Jones had long ago buried her wild-child
impulses and opted to be "safe," romantically
speaking. But one look at born rebel Jericho Bravo
and she began to wonder if her thrill-seeking side
was about to be revived. Because if ever there was
a man worth taking a chance on, there he was,
right within her grasp....

*Available in March
wherever books are sold.*

LARGER-PRINT BOOKS!

GET 2 FREE LARGER-PRINT NOVELS

PLUS 2 FREE GIFTS!

◆ HARLEQUIN®

INTRIGUE®

Breathtaking Romantic Suspense

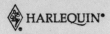 HARLEQUIN®

INTRIGUE

COMING NEXT MONTH

Available March 9, 2010

#1191 KILLER BODY
Bodyguard of the Month
Elle James

#1192 RAWHIDE RANGER
The Silver Star of Texas: Comanche Creek
Rita Herron

#1193 INDESTRUCTIBLE
Maximum Men
Cassie Miles

#1194 COLBY JUSTICE
Colby Agency: Under Siege
Debra Webb

#1195 COWBOY DELIRIUM
Special Ops Texas + Colts Run Cross
Joanna Wayne

#1196 UNDER THE GUN
Thriller
HelenKay Dimon

HICNMBPA0210